Nursery Rhymes
and
Fairy Tales

Nursery Rhymes
and
Fairy Tales
Margaret Tarrant

TREASURE PRESS

First published in Great Britain by Ward Lock Ltd
as two volumes: *Nursery Rhymes* and *Fairy Tales*

This edition published by Treasure Press
59 Grosvenor Street
London W1

Reprinted 1983, 1984, 1987

© 1978 Ward Lock Ltd

ISBN 0 907407 51 X

Printed in Czechoslovakia

50450/6

Contents

NURSERY RHYMES

FAIRY TALES

Nursery Rhymes

HUMPTY Dumpty sat on a wall,
Humpty Dumpty had a great fall;
Not all the king's horses, nor all the king's men
Could set Humpty Dumpty together again.

MONDAY'S child is fair of face,
Tuesday's child is full of grace,
Wednesday's child is full of woe,
Thursday's child has far to go,
Friday's child is loving and giving,
Saturday's child works hard for its living.
But the child that is born on the Sabbath Day
Is bonny, and blithe, and good, and gay.

OLD Mother Hubbard she went to the cupboard
  To get her poor dog a bone,
But when she got there the cupboard was bare,
And so the poor dog had none.

        She went to the baker's
        To buy him some bread;
        But when she came back
        The poor dog was dead.

        She went to the joiner's
        To buy him a coffin;
        But when she came back
        The poor dog was laughing.

        She took a clean dish
        To get him some tripe;
        But when she came back
        He was smoking a pipe.

        She went to the fishmonger's
        To buy him some fish,
        And when she came back
        He was licking the dish.

        She went to the tavern
        For white wine and red;
        But when she came back
        The dog stood on his head.

She went to the hatter's
To buy him a hat;
But when she came back
He was feeding the cat.

She went to the barber's
To buy him a wig;
But when she came back
He was dancing a jig.

She went to the fruiterer's
To buy him some fruit;
But when she came back
He was playing the flute.

She went to the tailor's
To buy him a coat;
But when she came back
He was riding a goat.

She went to the cobbler's
To buy him some shoes;
But when she came back
He was reading the news.

She went to the seamstress
To buy him some linen;
But when she came back
The dog was spinning.

The dame made a curtsey,
The dog made a bow;
The dame said, 'Your servant,'
The dog said, 'Bow, wow!'

HOT cross buns! hot cross buns!
One a penny, two a penny,
Hot cross buns!
If you have no daughters
Give them to your sons;
One a penny, two a penny
Hot cross buns.

LADY bird, lady bird, fly away home,
Your house is on fire, your children all gone;
All but one, and her name is Ann,
And she crept under the pudding pan.

THIRTY days hath September,
April, June, and November;
February has twenty-eight alone,
All the rest have thirty-one,
Excepting Leap-year, that's the time
When February's days are twenty-nine.

JACK and Jill went up the hill
To fetch a pail of water;
Jack fell down and cracked his crown,
And Jill came tumbling after.

Then up Jack got, and home did trot,
As fast as he could caper.
They put him to bed and plaster'd his head
With vinegar and brown paper.

THIS is the house that Jack built.
This is the malt
That lay in the house
That Jack built.

This is the rat
That ate the malt
That lay in the house
That Jack built.

This is the cat that killed the rat
That ate the malt
That lay in the house that Jack built.

This is the dog that worried the cat
That killed the rat that ate the malt
That lay in the house that Jack built.

This is the cow with the crumpled horn
That tossed the dog that worried the cat
That killed the rat that ate the malt
That lay in the house that Jack built.

This is the maiden all forlorn
That milked the cow with the crumpled horn
That tossed the dog that worried the cat
That killed the rat that ate the malt
That lay in the house that Jack built.

This is the man all tattered and torn
That kissed the maiden all forlorn
That milked the cow with the crumpled horn
That tossed the dog that worried the cat
That killed the rat that ate the malt
That lay in the house that Jack built.

This is the priest all shaven and shorn
That married the man all tattered and torn
That kissed the maiden all forlorn
That milked the cow with the crumpled horn
That tossed the dog that worried the cat
That killed the rat that ate the malt
That lay in the house that Jack built.

This is the cock that crowed in the morn
That waked the priest all shaven and shorn
That married the man all tattered and torn
That kissed the maiden all forlorn
That milked the cow with the crumpled horn
That tossed the dog that worried the cat
That killed the rat that ate the malt
That lay in the house that Jack built.

This is the farmer that sowed the corn
That fed the cock that crowed in the morn
That waked the priest all shaven and shorn
That married the man all tattered and torn
That kissed the maiden all forlorn
That milked the cow with the crumpled horn
That tossed the dog that worried the cat
That killed the rat that ate the malt
That lay in the house that Jack built.

PAT-a-cake, pat-a-cake, baker's man!
Make me a cake as fast as you can;
Pat it, and prick it, and mark it with B,
Put it in the oven for Baby and me.

THE brave old Duke of York
  He had ten thousand men;
He marched them up a very big hill,
Then marched them down again.
And when they were up they were up—up—up—
And when they were down they were down—
  down—down—
And when they were only half-way up they
  were neither up nor down.

DIDDLE, diddle, dumpling, my son John
  Went to bed with his trousers on;
One shoe off, the other shoe on;
Diddle, diddle, dumpling, my son John.

THERE was a crooked man, and he went a crooked mile,
  He found a crooked sixpence against a crooked stile:
He bought a crooked cat, which caught a crooked mouse,
And they all lived together in a little crooked house.

IF all the world was apple pie,
  And all the sea was ink,
And all the trees were bread and cheese,
What should we have to drink?
It's enough to make an old man
Scratch his head and think.

THE lion and the unicorn
  Fought for the crown;
The lion beat the unicorn
  Up and down the town.
Some gave them white bread,
  And some gave them brown
Some gave them plum cake
  And sent them out of town.

HICKETY, pickety, my black hen,
  She lays eggs for gentlemen;
Sometimes nine, sometimes ten,
  Hickety, pickety, my black hen.

SING a Song of Sixpence,
  A pocket full of rye;
Four-and-twenty blackbirds
  Baked in a pie.

When the pie was opened,
  The birds began to sing;
Was not that a dainty dish
  To set before the King?

The King was in the counting-house,
  Counting out his money;
The Queen was in the parlour,
  Eating bread and honey;

The maid was in the garden,
  Hanging out the clothes;
When down came a little bird
  And snapped off her nose!

I LOVE little pussy,
  Her coat is so warm,
And if I don't hurt her,
  She'll do me no harm;
So I'll not pull her tail,
  Nor drive her away,
But pussy and I
  Together will play.

AS I was going to sell my eggs,
  I met a man with bandy legs,
Bandy legs and crooked toes,
I tripped up his heels, and he fell on his nose.

PLEASE to remember the Fifth of November,
  Gunpowder treason plot.
I see no reason why gunpowder treason
  Should ever be forgot.

OH, where, oh, where is my little dog gone?
   Oh, where, oh, where can he be?
With his ears cut short and his tail cut long,
Oh, where, oh, where is he?

FOUR-and-twenty tailors went to kill a snail,
   The best man among them durst not touch her tail;
She put out her horns like a little Kyloe cow:
Run, tailors, run! or she'll kill you all e'en now.

BLOW, wind, blow! and go, mill, go!
   That the miller may grind his corn;
   That the baker may take it,
   And into rolls make it,
And bring us some hot in the morn.

THREE blind mice, three blind mice,
   See how they run! See how they run!
They all ran after the farmer's wife,
   Who cut off their tails with a carving knife.
Did ever you see such a thing in your life
   As three blind mice?

THERE was a little girl
  Who wore a little curl,
   Right in the middle of her forehead;
When she was good, she was very, very good,
  And when she was bad, she was horrid.

DICKORY, dickory, dare,
  The pig flew up in the air;
The man in brown soon brought him down,
   Dickory, dickory, dare.

TOM, Tom, the piper's son,
  Stole a pig, and away he run.
The pig was eat, and Tom was beat,
And Tom went roaring down the street.

THE north wind doth blow,
   And we shall have snow,
And what will poor Robin do then?
   Poor thing!

He'll sit in the barn,
And keep himself warm,
And hide his head under his wing.
Poor thing!

SNEEZE on Monday, sneeze for danger;
   Sneeze on Tuesday, kiss a stranger;
Sneeze on Wednesday, get a letter;
Sneeze on Thursday, something better;
Sneeze on Friday, sneeze for sorrow;
Sneeze on Saturday, see your sweetheart tomorrow.

LITTLE Bo-peep has lost her sheep,
    And can't tell where to find them;
Leave them alone, and they'll come home,
    And bring their tails behind them.

Little Bo-peep fell fast asleep,
    And dreamt she heard them bleating;
But when she awoke, she found it a joke,
    For they were still a-fleeting.

Then up she took her little crook,
    Determined for to find them
She found them indeed, but it made her heart bleed,
    For they'd left their tails behind them.

It happened one day, as Bo-peep did stray
    Over a meadow hard by,
That there she espied their tails side by side,
    All hung on a tree to dry.

She heaved a sigh, and gave by and by
    Each careless sheep a banging;
And as for the rest, she thought it was best
    Just to leave the tails a-hanging.

'WHO killed Cock Robin?'
  'I,' said the sparrow,
  'With my bow and arrow,
I killed Cock Robin.'

'Who saw him die?'
  'I,' said the fly,
  'With my little eye,
I saw him die.'

'Who caught his blood?'
  'I,' said the fish,
  'With my little dish,
I caught his blood.'

'Who'll make his shroud?'
  'I,' said the beetle,
  'With my thread and needle,
I'll make his shroud.'

'Who'll be the clerk?'
  'I,' said the lark,
  'If it's not in the dark,
I'll be the clerk.'

'Who'll be chief mourner?'
  'I,' said the dove,
  'I'll mourn for my love,
I'll be chief mourner.'

'Who'll dig his grave?'
  'I,' said the owl,
  'With my little trowel,
I'll dig his grave.'

'Who'll be the parson?'
  'I,' said the rook,
  'With my little book,
I'll be the parson.'

'Who'll toll the bell?'
  'I,' said the Bull,
  'Because I can pull,
I'll pull the bell.'

All the birds in the air
  Fell a-sighing and a-sobbing,
When they heard the bell toll
  For poor Cock Robin.

POLLY, put the kettle on,
  Polly, put the kettle on,
Polly, put the kettle on,
  We'll all have tea.

Sukey, take it off again,
Sukey, take it off again,
Sukey, take it off again,
  They've all gone away.

GOOSEY, goosey, gander, where shall I wander?
  Upstairs and downstairs, and in my lady's chamber.
There I met an old man, who would not say his prayers,
I took him by the left leg, and threw him down the stairs.

WHEN the wind is in the east,
  'Tis neither good for man nor beast;
When the wind is in the north,
The skilful fisher goes not forth;
When the wind is in the south,
It blows the bait in the fishes' mouth;
When the wind is in the west,
Then 'tis at the very best.

SEE-saw, Margery Daw,
　Jacky shall have a new master;
And he shall have but a penny a day,
　Because he can't work any faster.

BAA, baa, black sheep, have you any wool?
　Yes, sir; yes, sir, three bags full:
One for my master, one for my dame,
And one for the little boy who lives down the lane.

LUCY Locket lost her pocket;
　Kitty Fisher found it;
There was not a penny in it,
But a ribbon round it.

HUSH-a-bye, Baby, on the tree top,
When the wind blows the cradle will rock;
When the bough breaks the cradle will fall,
Down will come baby, and cradle, and all.

TWINKLE, twinkle, little star,
How I wonder what you are!
Up above the world so high,
Like a diamond in the sky!

When the blazing sun is gone,
When he nothing shines upon,
Then you show your little light,
Twinkle, twinkle all the night.

Then the traveller in the dark
Thanks you for your little spark.
He could not tell which way to go,
If you did not twinkle so.

In the dark blue sky you keep,
And often through my curtains peep;
For you never shut your eye,
Till the sun is in the sky.

LITTLE Boy Blue, come blow your horn!
The sheep's in the meadow, the cow's in the corn.
Where's the boy that looks after the sheep?
He's under the haycock, fast asleep.
Will you wake him? No, not I;
For if I do, he'll be sure to cry.

LITTLE Polly Flinders
Sat among the cinders,
Warming her pretty little toes!
Her mother came and caught her
And whipped her little daughter,
For spoiling her nice new clothes.

SEE-saw, Sacradown,
Which is the way to London Town?
One foot up, and the other down,
That is the way to London Town.

'WHERE are you going to, my pretty maid?'
'I'm going a-milking, sir,' she said.

'May I go with you, my pretty maid?'
'You're kindly welcome, sir,' she said.

'What is your father, my pretty maid?'
'My father's a farmer, sir,' she said.

'What is your fortune, my pretty maid?'
'My face is my fortune, sir,' she said.

'Then I can't marry you, my pretty maid!'
'Nobody asked you, sir!' she said.

ONE misty, moisty morning,
    When cloudy was the weather,
I met a little old man
    Clothed all in leather;
With cap under his chin,
    How do you do, and how do you do,
And how do you do again?

TWEEDLE-dum and Tweedle-dee
    Resolved to have a battle,
For Tweedle-dum said Tweedle-dee
    Had spoiled his nice new rattle.
Just then flew by a monstrous crow,
    As big as a tar-barrel,
Which frightened both the heroes so,
    They quite forgot their quarrel.

HANDY Spandy, Jack-a-dandy,
    Loved plum-cake and sugar candy;
He bought some at a grocer's shop,
And out he came, hop, hop, hop.

I HAD a little nut tree, nothing would it bear
But a silver nutmeg and a golden pear;
The King of Spain's daughter came to visit me,
And all was because of my little nut tree.
I skipped over water, I danced over sea,
And all the birds in the air couldn't catch me.

ONE, two, buckle my shoe;
Three, four, knock at the door;
Five, six, pick up sticks;
Seven, eight, lay them straight;
Nine, ten, a good fat hen;
Eleven, twelve, dig and delve;
Thirteen, fourteen, maids are courting;
Fifteen, sixteen, maids in the kitchen;
Seventeen, eighteen, maids are waiting;
Nineteen, twenty, my plate's empty.

JACK Sprat could eat no fat,
His wife could eat no lean;
And so betwixt them both, you see,
They lick'd the platter clean.

DAME, get up and bake your pies,
  Bake your pies, bake your pies;
Dame, get up and bake your pies,
On Christmas-day in the morning.

Dame, what makes your maidens lie,
Maidens lie, maidens lie;
Dame, what makes your maidens lie,
On Christmas-day in the morning?

Dame, what makes your ducks to die,
Ducks to die, ducks to die;
Dame, what makes your ducks to die,
On Christmas-day in the morning?

Their wings are cut and they cannot fly,
Cannot fly, cannot fly;
Their wings are cut, and they cannot fly,
On Christmas-day in the morning.

OLD King Cole was a merry old soul,
  And a merry old soul was he;
He called for his pipe, he called for his glass,
And he called for his fiddlers three.

Every fiddler he had a fine fiddle,
And a very fine fiddle had he;
Twee-tweedle-dee, tweedle-dee, went the fiddlers.
Oh, there's none so rare as can compare
With King Cole and his fiddlers three!

I SAW a ship a-sailing,
  A-sailing on the sea;
And, oh! it was all laden
  With pretty things for thee!

There were comfits in the cabin,
  And apples in the hold;
The sails were all of silk,
  And the masts were made of gold.

LITTLE Tom Tucker, sing for your supper.
What shall he sing for? White bread and butter.
How shall he cut it without any knife?
How shall he marry without any wife?

THREE little kittens they lost their mittens,
 And they began to cry
'Oh, mammy dear, we sadly fear
 That we have lost our mittens.'
'Lost your mittens? You naughty kittens!
 Then you shall have no pie!'
  Miaow, miaow, miaow,
  Miaow, miaow, miaow.

Three little kittens they found their mittens,
 And they began to cry
'Oh, mammy dear, see here, see here,
 See, we have found our mittens.'
'Found your mittens! You little kittens!
 Then you shall have some pie!'
  Miaow, miaow, miaow,
  Miaow, miaow, miaow.

The three little kittens put on their mittens,
 And soon ate up the pie.
'Oh, mammy dear, we sadly fear
 That we have soiled our mittens.'
'Soiled your mittens! You naughty kittens!'
 Then they began to sigh,
  Miaow, miaow, miaow,
  Miaow, miaow, miaow.

The three little kittens they washed their mittens
 And hung them out to dry.
'Oh, mammy dear, look here, look here,
 'See, we have washed our mittens!'
'What! Washed your mittens! You darling kittens!
 But I smell a rat close by!'
  Miaow, miaow, miaow,
  Miaow, miaow, miaow.

PEASE pudding hot,
  Pease pudding cold,
Pease pudding in the pot,
  Nine days old.

Some like it hot,
  Some like it cold,
Some like it in the pot,
  Nine days old.

THERE was a little man, and he had a little gun
   And his bullets were made of lead, lead, lead;
He went to the brook, and saw a little duck,
   And shot it through the head, head, head.

He carried it home to his old wife Joan,
   And bade her a fire to make, make, make;
To roast the little duck, while he went to the brook,
   To shoot and kill the drake, drake, drake.

   The little drake was swimming,
   With his little curly tail,
And the little man made it his mark, mark, mark:
   He let off his gun,
   But he fired too soon,
And away flew the drake with a quack, quack, quack.

THERE was an old woman, as I've heard tell,
    She went to market, her eggs for to sell;
She went to market all on a market-day,
And she fell asleep on the king's highway.

There came by a pedlar whose name was Stout;
He cut her petticoats all round about;
He cut her petticoats up to the knees,
Which made the old woman to shiver and freeze.

When this little woman first did wake,
She began to shiver and she began to shake;
She began to wonder and she began to cry,
'Oh! deary, deary me, this is none of I!

'But if it be I, as I do hope it be,
I've a little dog at home, and he'll know me;
If it be I, he'll wag his little tail,
And if it be not I, he'll loudly bark and wail.'

Home went the little woman all in the dark;
Up got the little dog and he began to bark;
He began to bark, so she began to cry
'Oh! deary, deary me, this is none of I!'

ELIZABETH, Elspeth, Betsy and Bess
They all went together to seek a bird's nest.
They found a bird's nest with five eggs in,
They all took one, and left four in.

MATTHEW, Mark, Luke and John,
Bless the bed that I lie on!
Four corners to my bed,
Four angels round my head:
One to watch, one to pray,
And two to bear my soul away!

THERE was a man of Newington, and he
was wondrous wise,
He jump'd into a bramble bush and scratch'd
out both his eyes.
And when he saw his eyes were out, with all
his might and main
He jump'd into another bush, and scratch'd
them in again.

RIDE a cock-horse to Banbury Cross,
To see a fine lady upon a white horse;
With rings on her fingers and bells on her toes
She shall have music wherever she goes.

WEE Willie Winkie runs through the town,
  Upstairs and downstairs in his night-gown,
Tapping at the window, crying through the lock,
'Are the babes in their beds,
For it's now ten o'clock?'

'Hey! Willie Winkie,
Are you coming then?
The cat's singing purrie
To the sleeping hen;
The dog is lying on the floor
And does not even peep;
But here's a wakeful laddie
That will not fall asleep.

'Anything but sleep, you rogue!
Glowering like the moon;
Rattling in an iron jug
With an iron spoon;

Rumbling, tumbling all about,
Crowing like a cock,
Screaming like I don't know what,
Waking sleeping folk.

'Hey! Willie Winkie,
Can't you keep him still?
Wriggling off a body's knee
Like a very eel;
Pulling at the cat's ear,
As she drowsy hums—
Hey, Willie Winkie!
See!—there he comes!

Wearied is the mother
That has a restless wean,
A wee, stumpy bairnie,
Heard whene'er he's seen—
That has a battle aye with sleep
Before he'll close an e'e;
But a kiss from off his rosy lips
Gives strength anew to me.

ONCE I saw a little bird
    Come hop, hop, hop;
So I cried, 'Little bird,
Will you stop, stop, stop?'
I was going to the window,
To say, 'How do you do?'
But he shook his little tail
And far away he flew.

BABY, baby bunting,
  Daddy's gone a-hunting,
To get a little rabbit's skin
To wrap his Baby Bunting in.

MARY had a little lamb,
Its fleece was white as snow;
And everywhere that Mary went
The lamb was sure to go.

It followed her to school one day:
That was against the rule;
It made the children laugh and play
To see a lamb at school.

And so the teacher turned it out,
But still it lingered near,
And waited patiently about
Till Mary did appear.

And then it ran to her and laid
Its head upon her arm,
As if it said, 'I'm not afraid—
You'll keep me from all harm.'

'What makes the lamb love Mary so?'
The eager children cry.
'Why, Mary loves the lamb, you know,'
The teacher did reply.

HALF a pound of tuppeny rice,
    Half a pound of treacle;
That's the way the money goes—
    Pop goes the weasel!

GIRLS and boys, come out to play,
    The moon doth shine as bright as day;
Come with a whistle, come with a call,
Come with a good will, or come not at all.

Leave your supper, leave your slate,
And come to your playfellows in the street;
Come with a shout, and come with a bound,
And dance in the moonlight round and round.

Up the ladder, and down the wall,
A halfpenny roll will serve us all;
You'll find milk, and I'll find flour,
And we'll have a pudding in half-an-hour.

DOCTOR Foster went to Gloster,
    In a shower of rain;
He stepped in a puddle, up to the middle,
    And never went there again.

ELSIE Marley is grown so fine
  She won't get up to feed the swine,
But lies in bed till eight or nine,
And surely she does take her time.

Do you ken Elsie Marley, honey?
The wife who sells the barley, honey?
She won't get up to feed her swine,
And do you ken Elsie Marley, honey?

MY Lady Wind, my Lady Wind,
Went round about the house to find
   A chink to get her foot in.
She tried the keyhole in the door,
She tried the crevice in the floor,
   And drove the chimney soot in.

And then one night when it was dark,
She blew up such a tiny spark
   That all the house was pothered.
From it she raised up such a flame
As flamed away to Belting Lane,
   And White Cross folks were smothered.

And thus when once, my little dears,
A whisper reaches itching ears,
   The same will come you'll find.
Take my advice, restrain the tongue,
Remember what old nurse has sung
   Of busy Lady Wind.

DAFFY-down-dilly has come up to town,
In a yellow petticoat and a green gown.

THERE was an old woman toss'd up in a basket,
  Ninety times as high as the moon;
Where she was going, I couldn't but ask it,
For in her hand she carried a broom.

'Old woman, old woman, old woman,' quoth I,
'O whither, O whither, O whither so high?'
  'To brush the cobwebs off the sky!'
'Shall I go with thee?'
  'Ay, by and by.'

PUSSY-cat, pussy-cat, where have you been?
  I've been to London to see the Queen.
Pussy-cat, pussy-cat, what did you there?
I caught a little mouse under her chair.

MARY, Mary, quite contrary,
How does your garden grow?
With cockle shells and silver bells
And cowslips all in a row.

LONDON Bridge is broken down,
  Dance o'er my Lady Lee;
London Bridge is broken down,
  With a gay lady.

How shall we build it up again?
  Dance o'er my Lady Lee;
How shall we build it up again?
  With a gay lady.

Build it up with silver and gold,
  Dance o'er my Lady Lee;
Build it up with silver and gold,
  With a gay lady.

Silver and gold will be stole away,
  Dance o'er my Lady Lee;
Silver and gold will be stole away,
  With a gay lady.

Build it up again with iron and steel,
  Dance o'er my Lady Lee;
Build it up with iron and steel,
  With a gay lady.

Iron and steel will bend and break,
Dance o'er my Lady Lee;
Iron and steel will bend and break,
   With a gay lady.

Build it up with wood and clay,
   Dance o'er my Lady Lee;
Build it up with wood and clay,
   With a gay lady.

Wood and clay will wash away,
   Dance o'er my Lady Lee;
Wood and clay will wash away,
   With a gay lady.

Build it up with stone so strong,
   Dance o'er my Lady Lee;
Huzza! 'twill last for ages long,
   With a gay lady.

RUB a dub dub,
  Three men in a tub;
And who do you think they be?
The butcher, the baker,
The candlestick-maker;
Turn 'em out, knaves all three!

OLD Mother Goose,
    When she wanted to wander,
Would ride through the air
    On a very fine gander.

Mother Goose had a house,
    'Twas built in a wood,
Where an owl at the door
    As sentinel stood.

She had a son Jack,
    A plain-looking lad,
He was not very good,
    Nor yet very bad.

She sent him to market,
    A live goose he bought;
'Here, mother,' says he,
    'It will not go for nought.'

Jack's goose and her gander
    Soon grew very fond,
They'd both eat together
    And swim in one pond.

Jack found one morning,
    As I have been told,
His goose had laid him
    An egg of pure gold.

Jack ran to his mother,
    The news for to tell;
She called him a good boy,
    And said it was well.

Jack sold his gold egg
    To a merchant untrue,
Who cheated him out of
    The half of his due.

Then Jack went a-courting
    A lady so gay,
As fair as the lily,
    And sweet as the may.

The rascally merchant
    Soon came at his back,
And began to belabour
    The sides of poor Jack.

He threw the gold egg
    In the midst of the sea;
But Jack he jumped in,
    And got it back presently.

The merchant then vowed
    The goose he would kill,
Resolving at once
    His pockets to fill.

Jack's mother came in,
    And caught the goose soon,
And, mounting its back,
    Flew up to the moon.

THERE was an old woman who lived in a shoe;
  She had so many children she didn't know what to do.
She gave them some broth without any bread;
Then whipped them all soundly and put them to bed.

DING, dong, bell,
Pussy's in the well
Who put her in?
Little Tommy Green.
Who pulled her out?
Little Tommy Stout.
What a naughty boy was that
To drown poor pussy cat,
Who never did him any harm,
But killed the mice in father's barn.

AS I was going to St Ives,
I met a man with seven wives,
Every wife had seven sacks,
Every sack had seven cats,
Every cat had seven kits:
Kits, cats, sacks, and wives,
How many were there going to St Ives?

A apple pie,
B bit it,
C cut it,
D dealt it,
E eat (ate) it,
F fought for it,
G got it,
H had it,
I inked it,
J joined it,
K kept it,
L longed for it,
M mourned for it,
N nodded at it,
O opened it,
P peeped in it,
Q quartered it,
R ran for it,
S stole it,
T took it,
V viewed it,
W wanted it,
X, **Y**, **Z**, and ampersand
All wished for a piece in hand.

H EY, diddle, diddle, the cat and the fiddle,
The cow jumped over the moon;
The little dog laughed to see such sport,
While the dish ran away with the spoon.

I SAW three ships come sailing by,
  Come sailing by, come sailing by;
I saw three ships come sailing by,
  On New Year's Day in the morning.

And what do you think was in them then?
Was in them then, was in them then?
And what do you think was in them then,
  On New Year's Day in the morning?

Three pretty girls were in them then,
Were in them then, were in them then;
Three pretty girls were in them then,
  On New Year's Day in the morning.

And one could whistle, and one could sing,
And one could play on the violin;
Such joy there was at my wedding,
  On New Year's Day in the morning.

LAVENDER'S blue, dilly, dilly, lavender's green;
  When I am king, dilly, dilly, you shall be queen;
Call up your men, dilly, dilly, set them to work:
Some to the plough, dilly, dilly, some to the cart,
Some to make hay, dilly, dilly, some to thresh corn;
Whilst you and I, dilly, dilly, keep ourselves warm.

THE man in the moon
  Came tumbling down,
And asked his way to Norwich:
    He went by the south,
    And burnt his mouth
With supping cold pease porridge.

HOW many miles to Babylon?
  Three-score miles and ten.
Can I get there by candle-light?
    Yes, and back again.
If your heels are nimble and light,
You may get there by candle-light.

LITTLE Jack Horner
Sat in a corner,
Eating a Christmas pie;
He put in his thumb,
And pulled out a plum,
And cried 'What a good boy am I!'

GAY go up and gay go down,
To ring the bells of London town.

Oranges and lemons,
Say the bells of St Clement's.

Bull's eyes and targets,
Say the bells of St Marg'ret's.

Brickbats and tiles,
Say the bells of St Giles'.

Halfpence and farthings,
Say the bells of St Martin's.

Pancakes and fritters,
Say the bells of St Peter's.

Two sticks and an apple,
Say the bells of Whitechapel.

Pokers and tongs,
Say the bells of St John's.

Kettles and pans,
Say the bells of St Ann's.

Old Father Baldpate,
Say the slow bells of Aldgate.

You owe me ten shillings,
Say the bells of St Helen's.

When will you pay me?
Say the bells of Old Bailey.

When I grow rich,
Say the bells of Shoreditch.

Pray when will that be?
Say the bells of Stepney.

I do not know,
Says the great bell of Bow.

Here comes a candle to light you to bed,
Here comes a chopper to chop off your head.

HARK! hark! the dogs do bark;
　The beggars are coming to town:
Some in jags, and some in rags,
　And some in velvet gown.

TOM, Tom, the piper's son,
  Learnt to play when he was young,
But the only tune that he could play
Was 'Over the hills and far away';
Over the hills, and a great way off,
And the wind will blow my top-knot off.

Now Tom with his pipe made such a noise,
That he pleased both the girls and boys,
And they stopped to hear him play
'Over the hills and far away'.

Tom on his pipe did play with such skill,
That those who heard him could never keep still;
Whenever they heard they began for to dance—
Even pigs on their hind legs would after him prance.

As Dolly was milking her cow one day,
Tom took out his pipe and began for to play;
So Doll and the cow danced 'the Cheshire round',
Till the pail was broke, and the milk ran on the ground.

He met old Dame Trot with a basket of eggs,
He used his pipe and she used her legs;
She danced about till the eggs were all broke,
She began for to fret, but he laughed at the joke.

He saw a cross fellow was beating an ass,
Heavy laden with pots, pans, dishes and glass,
He took out his pipe and played them a tune,
And the jackass's load was lightened full soon.

CAN you make me a cambric shirt,
   Parsley, sage, rosemary and thyme,
Without any seam or needlework?
And you shall be a true lover of mine.

Can you wash it in yonder well,
Parsley, sage, rosemary and thyme,
Which never sprung water, nor rain ever fell?
   And you shall be a true lover of mine.

Can you dry it on yonder thorn,
   Parsley, sage, rosemary and thyme,
Which never bore blossom since Adam was born?
   And you shall be a true lover of mine.

Now you have asked me questions three,
   Parsley, sage, rosemary and thyme,
I hope you'll answer as many for me,
   And you shall be a true lover of mine.

Can you find me an acre of land,
  Parsley, sage, rosemary and thyme,
Between the salt water and the sea-sand?
  And you shall be a true lover of mine.

Can you plough it with a ram's horn,
  Parsley, sage, rosemary and thyme,
And sow it all over with one peppercorn?
  And you shall be a true lover of mine.

Can you reap it with a sickle of leather,
  Parsley, sage, rosemary and thyme,
And bind it up with a peacock's feather?
  And you shall be a true lover of mine.

When you have done and finished your work,
  Parsley, sage, rosemary and thyme,
Then come to me for your cambric shirt,
  And you shall be a true lover of mine.

THE Queen of Hearts
   She made some tarts,
All on a summer's day;
The Knave of Hearts
He stole the tarts,
And with them ran away.
The King of Hearts
Called for the tarts,
And beat the Knave full sore;
The Knave of Hearts
Brought back the tarts,
And said he'd ne'er steal more.

HERE we go round the mulberry bush,
The mulberry bush, the mulberry bush,
Here we go round the mulberry bush,
On a cold and frosty morning.

This is the way we wash our hands,
Wash our hands, wash our hands,
This is the way we wash our hands
On a cold and frosty morning.

This is the way we wash our clothes,
Wash our clothes, wash our clothes,
This is the way we wash our clothes
On a cold and frosty morning.

This is the way we go to school,
Go to school, go to school,
This is the way we go to school
On a cold and frosty morning.

This is the way we come out of school,
Come out of school, come out of school,
This is the way we come out of school
On a cold and frosty morning.

THIS little pig went to market;
   This little pig stayed at home;
This little pig had roast beef;
This little pig had none;
This little pig cried 'Wee, wee, wee!'
   All the way home.

HICKORY, Dickory, Dock,
   The mouse ran up the clock;
The clock struck one,
The mouse ran down;
Hickory, Dickory, Dock.

JACK, be nimble,
   Jack, be quick,
And Jack, jump over the candlestick.

RING-a-ring of roses,
A pocket full of posies.
Tishoo! Tishoo!
We all fall down.

Fairy Tales

The Three Bears

O NCE upon a time there lived in a pretty little house in the midst of a great forest three bears.

The first was a Big Bear, with a big head, big paws, and a big gruff voice.

The second was a Middling-sized Bear, with a middling-sized head, a middling-sized body, and a voice that was neither very loud nor very soft.

The third was a wee little Baby Bear, with a wee little head, a wee little body, and a teeny-weeny voice between a whine and a squeak.

Now although the home of these three bears was rather rough, they had in it all the things they wanted. There was a big chair for the Big Bear to sit in, a big porridge-bowl from which he could eat his breakfast, and a big bed, very strongly made, on which he could sleep at night. The Middling-sized Bear had a middling-sized porridge-bowl, with a chair and a bed to match. For the Little Bear there was a nice little chair, a neat little bed, and a porridge-bowl that held just enough to satisfy a little bear's appetite.

Near the house of the three bears lived a child whose name was Goldilocks. She was very pretty, with long curls of the brightest gold, that shone and glittered in the sunshine. She was round and plump, merry and light-hearted, always running and jumping about, and singing the whole day long. When Goldilocks laughed (and she was always laughing when she wasn't singing, and sometimes when she was), her laugh rang out with a clear silvery sound that was very pleasant to hear.

One day she ran off into the woods to gather flowers. When she had gone some way, she began to make wreaths and garlands of wild roses and honeysuckle, and scarcely thought at all of where she was going or of how she was to get back.

At last she came to a part of the forest where there was an open space in which no trees grew. There was a kind of pathway trampled across it, as if someone with broad heavy feet was used to walking there.

Following this for a short distance she came, much to her surprise, to a funny little house roughly made of wood. There was a hole in the wall of the house and Goldilocks peeped through to see if anyone was at home. She stood on tiptoe and strained her eyes till they ached; but the house seemed quite empty. The longer she peeped, the more she wanted to know who lived in this funny little house, and what kind of people they were, and, if the truth must be told, a good many other little girls would have been quite as inquisitive.

At last her wish to see the inside of the house became so strong that she could resist no longer: there seemed to be someone pushing her forward, while a voice called in her ear, 'Go in, Goldilocks, go in.' So, after a little more peeping, she opened the door very softly, and timidly walked right in.

But where were the bears at this time, and why were they not there to welcome their pretty little guest?

'Somebody has been at my porridge, and has eaten it all up,'
squeaked the Little Bear.

Every morning they used to get up early – wise bears as they were – and when the Middling-sized Bear, who was also the Mummy Bear, had cooked the porridge, she would say, if it was a fine morning:

'The porridge is too hot to eat just yet. We will go for a little walk, my dears. The fresh air will give us an appetite, and when we come back the porridge will be just right.'

And that is why the bears were not at home when Goldilocks walked into their house.

When she came into the bears' room, Goldilocks was surprised to see a big porridge-bowl, a middling-sized porridge-bowl, and a little porridge-bowl all standing on the table.

'Some of the people who live here must eat a good deal more than the others,' she thought. 'Whoever can want all the porridge that is in the big bowl? It looks very good. I wonder whether it is sweetened with sugar, or if they put salt into it. I'll just try a taste.'

So she put the great spoon into the big bowl, and ladled out some of the Big Bear's breakfast.

Now there was so much porridge in the Big Bear's bowl that it kept hot longer than the porridge in the middling-sized bowl and in the little bowl. When Goldilocks put the big spoon into her mouth – or rather all of it that she could get in – she drew back with a scream and danced with pain. For the porridge was very, very hot and burned her mouth, and Goldilocks did not like it at all.

'Whatever sort of person can eat such stuff?' she said.

So she tried the middling-sized bowl; and you may be sure she took good care to blow on the spoon before it went into her mouth. But she need not have been so careful, for the porridge was quite cold and sticky. So she stuck the spoon upright in the bowl, and wondered again whoever could eat such stuff.

Then she tried the little porridge-bowl; and the porridge in that was just right, neither too hot nor too cold, and with just the right quantity of sugar.

Having finished the first spoonful, Goldilocks thought she would try a second; and then, being still hungry, she had a third and a fourth and a fifth. By this time she could see the bottom of the bowl, so she thought she might as well look round for a comfortable chair in which to sit and finish all that was left.

First she scrambled up into the Big Bear's chair. It was cold and hard and much too high for her. Next she tried the Middling-sized Bear's chair, but that was just as bad the other way, too soft and bulging.

Then she caught sight of the teeny-tiny chair that belonged to the Little Bear. It cracked beneath her weight, but was just as comfy as ever a chair could be. So she sat in it and finished up the very last spoonful of porridge.

Then she began to feel very tired and sleepy and gave a great yawn. There was a crack, a groan, and a crash! Down went the bottom of the chair, for you see it was only made for a wee little bear to sit in.

Goldilocks felt a little frightened when she found herself on the floor, but soon got up, and, still being very sleepy, thought she would go upstairs and see if there was a bed to lie on.

A ladder stood in the middle of the room, and there was a hole in the ceiling above it. Goldilocks climbed the ladder and found, as she expected, that it led to the bedroom. It was a pretty little room, with pink and red roses peeping in at the open window, and in the middle were three beds – a big one, a middling-sized one, and a teeny-weeny one.

'They must be funny people in this house,' she thought, 'to have all their things of such different sizes!' She looked at the beds to see which she should rest upon, and tried the big bed first. It would not do at all – the pillow was hard and so big that it kept her head too high. The middling-sized bed was no better – it was so soft that she flopped right down in it. Then Goldilocks tried the little bed and that was just right – sweet and dainty, very white and very soft, with snowy sheets, a blue and white counterpane, and a pillow exactly the right height. So Goldilocks laid herself down, with her pretty head on the comfy pillow, and in a very few seconds fell fast asleep.

But before she dropped off to sleep, Goldilocks wondered a little what the people of the house, who owned the porridge-bowls, and the chairs, and the beds, would say if they knew she was there and what she had done.

Soon – very soon – there were sounds in the room below. A big heavy foot went bump – bump – bump; a middling-sized foot went tramp – tramp – tramp; and a tiny little foot went pit-pat – pit-pat – pit-pat. The three bears had come home to breakfast! And directly they came into the room they all three sniffed and sniffed and sniffed.

When the Big Bear came to his porridge-bowl, and found the spoon sticking upright, he knew at once that someone had meddled with it. So he gave an angry roar and growled in his big voice:

'SOMEBODY HAS BEEN AT MY PORRIDGE!'

At this the Middling-sized Bear ran across the room

'Somebody has been lying on *my* bed!' squeaked the Little
Bear. 'And she's lying on it still!'

to look at *her* breakfast; and when she found the spoon sticking up in *her* porridge-bowl, she cried out, though not so loudly as the Big Bear had done:

'SOMEBODY HAS BEEN AT MY PORRIDGE!'

Then the Little Bear ran to *his* porridge-bowl; and when he found all his porridge gone, and not even enough left for the spoon to stand upright in, he squeaked in a poor piteous little voice:

'*Somebody has been at my porridge, and has eaten it all up!*'

He tilted up his little porridge-bowl to show the others, stuffed his little fore-paws into his little eyes, and began to cry.

While the Little Bear cried, the Big Bear looked round and caught sight of his chair, on which Goldilocks had left the cushion all awry. This made him angrier still, and he growled:

'SOMEBODY HAS BEEN SITTING IN MY CHAIR!'

Then the Middling-sized Bear noticed that in the soft cushion of her chair was a hollow where Goldilocks had sat down. So she called out in her middling-sized voice:

'SOMEBODY HAS BEEN SITTING IN MY CHAIR!'

The Little Bear stopped crying for a moment and looked at *his* chair. Then he forgot all about the porridge, and called out in his squeaky little voice:

'*Somebody has been sitting in my chair, and has pushed the bottom right out of it!*'

The three bears all looked at one another in surprise. Whoever could have dared to do such things – in *their* house too!

'Some mortal has been here,' said the Big Bear.

'Yes,' said the Middling-sized Bear, sniffing around. 'Let's go upstairs.'

So the Big Bear went stumping up the ladder, with the Middling-sized Bear at his heels and the Little Bear last of all.

Goldilocks had tumbled the Big Bear's bolster in trying to make it low enough for her head. The Big Bear noticed it at once, and growled:

'SOMEBODY HAS BEEN LYING IN MY BED!'

And the Middling-sized Bear said in her middling-sized voice:

'SOMEBODY HAS BEEN LYING IN MY BED!'

Then the Little Bear saw something that made all the hair on his body stand on end.

There was the bed, all smooth and white; the counterpane was in its place and the pillow too; but on them, fast asleep, lay little Goldilocks. To make *quite* sure, he climbed on the end of the bed and looked over the rail. Then:

'*Somebody has been lying on my bed!*' squeaked the Little Bear. '*And she's lying on it still!*'

The Big Bear, the Middling-sized Bear, and the Little Bear all stood with their mouths wide open, staring in surprise at Goldilocks. Then the Big Bear gave a grunt; and the Middling-sized Bear gave a growl; and the Little Bear, who loved his little bed very much because it was so comfy, cried and cried and cried, and thought perhaps he would never be able to sleep on it any more.

The noise startled Goldilocks from her sleep. Up she jumped, and if she had wondered at seeing the three porridge-bowls, and the three chairs, and the three beds, you can fancy her surprise when she saw the Big

111

On and on Goldilocks ran, thinking every moment that she
heard the bears sniffing behind her.

Bear, and the Middling-sized Bear, and the Little Bear.

They all came forward at the same time, and Goldi-locks, terribly frightened, sprang from the teeny-weeny bed and with a single bound jumped clean through the open window.

She was lucky enough to fall on a nice soft flower-bed that the Big Bear had just dug. On and on she ran, through the forest, thinking every moment that she heard the bears sniffing behind her.

But if she could only have heard what the bears said, she would not have been at all frightened.

'I think she was rather a nice girl,' said the Big Bear in his big voice.

'So do I,' said the Middling-sized Bear in her middling-sized voice.

'And so do I,' said the Little Bear in his teeny-weeny voice, 'and I wished she had stopped to play with me.'

The Sleeping Beauty

ONCE upon a time there lived a King and Queen, who loved each other tenderly. The only drawback to their happiness was that they had no children; so when, after many years, a little daughter came to them you may be sure there were great rejoicings.

It was a beautiful little baby, with blue eyes and a fair skin; and it scarcely ever cried. The King and Queen were so pleased that they ordered a large sum of money to be given to the poor; and great preparations were at once made for the christening. Every fairy in the land was invited to act as a godmother to the little Princess, for her fond parents thought the fairies would be sure to shower gifts and graces upon her, as was the custom of fairies in those days.

But in sending out the cards of invitation a great mistake was made. One old fairy, of nasty temper, who was really a witch, was by accident left out. She had been travelling abroad, and the King's chamberlain did not know she had returned, or he would certainly have been on the safe side and sent her an invitation.

When the christening was over, all the guests passed into the great hall, where a splendid banquet was

served. The King and Queen made every effort to do
honour to their company; and each of the seven fairies
who had come as godmothers was provided with a plate
of pure gold to eat from, and a case containing a knife,
fork, and spoon, enriched with rubies and emeralds, as
a token of respect and gratitude. The feast had only just
begun when the cross old fairy came hobbling in, and
in a sulky tone demanded that room should be made for
her among the other fairies. This was done at once, and
she sat down to the table. But, as she had not been
invited or expected, no gold plate or jewelled knife and
fork had been provided for her. When·she was served
and saw that her things were not so good and costly as
those set before the other fairies, she fell into a great
rage and began muttering between her teeth that she
would be revenged.

Luckily, one of the fairies noticed these black looks
and, knowing the old hag's character, felt sure she
would cast some wicked spell over the innocent little
baby. So when the banquet was over, this good fairy
hid herself behind the tapestry hangings of the hall, so
that when the other fairies offered their gifts to the
Princess, she might come last and avert any mischief the
old hag might try to do.

As she stood there, the good fairy heard the other
fairies talking about the little child: one said what pretty
eyes it had; another admired its fat little hands, and
another its soft brown hair. And all the while the wicked
old hag stood apart, muttering to herself.

When the time came, the fairies went forward and
bestowed their gifts and good wishes on the little baby
Princess. The first promised her beauty, the second
cleverness, the third sweetness of temper, and so on

All the fairies in the land came to the christening.

until each had given her some good quality. Then it came to the turn of the wicked old hag to speak.

She walked into the middle of the hall, and stretching out her hand and shaking her head spitefully, exclaimed, 'My gift to the Princess is that she shall prick her finger with a spindle and die of the wound.'

All who heard were surprised and horrified at this wicked wish, and stood looking at the fairy, doubtful whether she could have spoken in earnest. But once more she stretched out her hand and, pointing to the baby Princess, repeated her words. Then, with a yell of laughter and a look of the deadliest spite, she vanished.

Everyone, from the King on the throne to the little scullion who peeped behind the door, felt inclined to weep as they realized the terrible fate in store for the babe. But at this moment the good fairy stepped from behind the tapestry and said in a gentle voice:

'Do not grieve, good friends, for things are not so bad as you imagine. The old fairy has spoken in hate and malice; but I can partly avert the effect of her anger, though not completely. Your daughter shall indeed pierce her hand with a spindle,' she continued, turning to the King and Queen; 'but she shall not die of the wound: she shall only be cast into a deep sleep. For a hundred years she will be insensible to everything around her, but at the appointed time the appointed person will come to wake her.' When the good fairy had thus spoken she and her sisters vanished, and the christening party broke up in sadness.

The King and Queen took great pains with the education of their little daughter, and as she grew up the effects of the fairy gifts were seen by all. Every day she became more beautiful and more clever; and, what was of even greater consequence, she was so kind and gentle that everyone loved and admired her. Nurses and governesses had no trouble with her, and even the great gruff house dog who lived in the kennel in the castle yard, and who barked at everyone else, would sniff, and wag his tail, and tumble with delight, directly the little Princess came in view. He would let her put garlands of flowers round his neck, and the more she pulled his ears the better he was pleased.

Remembering what the witch had said, the King was careful to have every spindle in the palace destroyed and forbade all his servants and subjects, under pain of instant death, to use one. Nobody was even to utter the word 'spindle'; and some people say the King even went so far as to discharge three of his footmen because they had spindle-shanks!

But, as you will shortly see, all this care was useless.

One day, when the Princess was just fifteen years old, the King and Queen left the palace almost for the first time since the birth of their daughter; for generally they preferred to stay at home, entertaining their lords and ladies, and the foreign guests who came to see them, in their own palace, as a king and queen ought to do. But on this occasion it happened that they were both compelled to go from home and would be absent for a day or two on important affairs of state. The Princess, left to herself, was rather at a loss to know how to spend the time. Having tired of books and music, and being in a restless mood, she thought she would explore the castle, and especially have a look at a number of holes and corners she had never before seen. Thus she came at last to the most ancient tower of the castle and, climbing by the dusty stairs to the top-most storey, came to a little room. Pushing open the door, which hung on a rusty and creaking hinge, she stopped in amazement. For seated on a low, old-fashioned stool in a corner of the room, and humming a tune in a funny, cracked voice, was an old woman, spinning with a distaff and spindle. The poor old creature had been allowed for years to live in this turret-room; and as she seldom left it, except to go to the royal kitchen to fetch the scraps of food that were allowed her, and as she was moreover very deaf, she had never heard of the King's edict, and did not dream, worthy soul, that she was doing wrong.

'What are you doing, goody?' asked the Princess.

'I am spinning, pretty lady,' was the reply, when at last the old dame understood the question.

'How pretty it looks!' said the Princess; 'I wish I could spin too. Will you let me try?'

The old dame of course had no idea that her visitor was the Princess, and she at once consented. The Princess took the distaff, but, never having handled such a thing before, was so awkward that in a moment she had pricked her finger. At once the fairy spell began to work. The Princess looked at her wound, uttered a little scream, and fell into a deep sleep.

The old woman, much alarmed, called lustily for help, and in a few moments the ladies-in-waiting and many of the servants came running up the stairs. When they learned what had happened there was a great commotion. One loosened the Princess's girdle; another sprinkled cold water on her face; another tried to revive her by rubbing her hands; and a fourth wetted her temples with scent. But all their efforts were vain.

There lay the Princess, beautiful as an angel, the colour still in her lips and cheeks, and her bosom

'I wish I could spin too,' said the Princess.
'Will you let me try?'

heaving, but her eyes were fast closed in a death-like sleep.

When the King and Queen came home they saw at once that there was no remedy but patience. The wicked fairy's curse had been fulfilled. But they did not entirely despair, for they remembered also what the good fairy had said, and knew that although they themselves would probably never again see their beloved child awake, she was not really dead.

The King gave orders that his daughter should be laid on a magnificent couch, covered with velvet and embroidery, in the best room of the palace, and that guards should be stationed at the chamber door night and day.

Feeling too sorrowful to remain in the palace, the King and Queen then went away to a distant part of the kingdom.

The very next day the good fairy, who was thousands of leagues away, heard of her godchild's misfortune, and rushed to the palace in her chariot, drawn by fiery dragons.

Invisible to all, she passed through the palace, touching with her wand as she went every living thing. Immediately a deep sleep fell on all she touched. Ladies-in-waiting, maids of honour, officers, gentle-men-in-waiting, cooks, scullions, guards, pages, porters, even the very horses in the stables and the cats in front of the fires fell asleep; and the strangest thing of all was that they all went to sleep in a moment, without having time to finish what they were about. The very spits before the kitchen fire ceased turning when they were only half way round, and the Princess's little lap-dog stood on only three legs.

In a few days a thick and thorny hedge grew up all round the place, and the forest trees intertwined their branches to form a wall that neither man nor beast could get through.

A hundred years is a very long time, and many things happen as the days roll on. The King died, and the Queen died, and, as they had no other children, the throne passed to another branch of the royal family. As year succeeded year the very existence of the castle was forgotten, except that now and then one peasant would tell another the tale of the christening of the beautiful Princess, to which all the great lords and ladies had been invited, and the fairies too; and how the Princess had vanished, no one knew whither, but was supposed to be lying asleep, on a bed of gold and silver, in a wonderful enchanted castle somewhere in the wood.

At last a century passed away.

One day the son of the reigning King was hunting in the woods, and went deeper into the forest than usual. Fancying he saw the turrets of a castle at a distance above the trees, he questioned his attendants, but they could tell him nothing. On passing through a neighbouring village he ordered his servants to make inquiries; but either the people knew nothing about the castle, or they were unwilling to tell. At last a very old peasant came forward and told the Prince the story of the enchanted palace. 'My father,' he added, 'told it to me when a boy, full fifty years ago; he said the people used often to talk of it when I was little. He said all the people in the castle had disappeared on a certain day, and the castle itself was lost to view; for the wood was too thick for anyone to get through; and it was said no one could enter till the appointed time. My father himself was young when it occurred, so that, to my thinking, the hundred years have nearly passed.'

These words of the old man set the Prince thinking deeply. He was fond of adventure, as most young princes are; and the more he thought about it, the more convinced he felt that it was up to him to solve the mystery. He went to sleep that night determined to try his fortune on the morrow.

Early next morning the Prince set out alone on his adventure. When he reached the wood he sprang from his horse and drew his sword to cut a path through the thick undergrowth. To his surprise, the branches gave way, and the brambles and thorns opened a passage as he proceeded. He noticed, however, that they closed behind him as dense as ever. Greatly wondering, he went on bravely till he reached the castle porch.

Here a company of musicians had been playing, and the King's fool, in his suit of motley, had been listening. All were fast asleep, and a man who had been singing had not even had time to shut his mouth.

Inside the gateway a hunting party had just arrived. All seemed to have turned to stone as they had ridden into the yard. Some had alighted, others were still in the saddle, but all alike were fast asleep, men and horses and dogs.

A little farther on sat a Court lady and a knight. The knight had been amusing himself and the lady with a tame raven. A page stood by them with refreshments on a tray, but these were still untouched.

What struck the Prince as much as anything was the deathless silence. Not a voice spoke, not a leaf stirred; the very air seemed to be motionless.

He went on through the lower or basement storey.

A groom stood fast asleep, his ear at a keyhole, a sly look of wisdom on his face.

The next room through which the Prince passed was the butler's. He had been arrested by the fairy's touch while in the very act of taking a glass of his master's choicest wine.

In another room was a scullery-maid, fast asleep, with a dish she had been wiping a hundred years before in her hand; by her fat and lazy appearance, the Prince thought it was perhaps not an uncommon occurrence for her to fall asleep over her work.

In the servants' hall the footmen and grooms were all fast asleep. One sat behind the door: he had been drawing on his boots when the fairy threw him into the enchanted sleep, and there he sat with one boot off and the other one on. In the great kitchen the chief cook sat in a chair before the fire, with the dripping-ladle in one hand and a sop in the other. One bite he had taken out of his sop, then sleep had come upon him, and he sat there, the very picture of contentment and repose. Never was there such a sleepy household since kings first kept castles and had servants to attend them.

A dozen or more turnspit dogs, little fellows with long bodies and short legs, had been employed in turning the wheel which kept the joints of meat and poultry moving round and round, as they roasted before the fire; but not a single spit was turning and the little dogs, one and all, were fast asleep.

In the passage, standing with his nose close to the ground, and watching intently, was the Queen's favourite cat, a Persian with a feathery tail. He had imagined, just a hundred years before, that he smelt a mouse somewhere near.

The Prince brushed aside the curtains, and there, on a
couch in the centre of a splendid room, lay the Princess.

At the end of a long passage the Prince came to a grand staircase, and at the head of this was a tall arched doorway, with a rich velvet curtain before it. He guessed that this doorway led to some room of importance; for above the door was a great crown and two flags drooped over the entrance. Here stood, too, a number of soldiers in full armour, with helmets, breast-plates, and tall spears. Very handsome and martial they looked; but each man's head had sunk upon his breast. And if the old Roman law had been put into force which pronounces death against every soldier found asleep at his post, the Princess's guards would have been executed to a man. Walking past them, the Prince brushed aside the curtains, and there, on a couch in the centre of the room, lay the Princess, as fresh and sweet and blooming as any Princess could possibly be. She looked, indeed, like a rosebud in a bed of leaves, and as if she had gone to sleep but an hour before.

The Prince could not restrain his admiration. Bending over her, he looked long and earnestly; and the longer he looked, the more he admired. Then he did what most men would have done; that is to say he gave her a kiss! At least that is the general belief, but as nobody saw, and the Princess never told, we cannot be quite sure.

Instantly there was a stir and a hum all through the castle. The enchantment was broken, and, with a great sigh of relief, men, women, children and animals all woke up. Outside the Princess's room a loud clash was heard, as of armed men dressing their ranks and clattering their weapons. The fat cook in the kitchen finished the sop from which he had taken only a bite; the butler drank the glass of wine he was about to pour out a hundred years before; the scullery-maid finished wiping the dish; the groom finished pulling on his boot; the Persian cat started again to go after the mouse he had sniffed at a hundred years before; and the little dogs resumed their work of turning the spits in front of the kitchen fire.

Exactly what the Prince said to the Princess has never been told, but of course when she saw him she knew the spell had been broken, and as he was as handsome a Prince as a maid could wish for, they were soon on the best of terms.

When the Prince presently appeared, leading the beautiful Princess by the hand, you may be sure the guards were wide awake. Every man among them stood at his post, his pike firmly grasped in his right hand, his head well up. The maidens of the castle strewed flowers in the path of the happy pair, and there was general rejoicing.

The wedding was the grandest that had been known for a hundred years. The Princess rather hoped the good fairies would come to the ceremony, as they had come to the christening, only, as it was possible the bad fairy would come with them, no formal invitations were sent. But as the Prince and Princess lived happily together for many years, with scarcely a wry word the whole time, we may be fairly sure the fairies knew all about them and still looked after their beautiful god-child.

Tom Thumb

LONG, long ago, in the days of good King Arthur,
lived a very wonderful magician and enchanter,
known as Merlin. One day, while on a long journey,
feeling hungry and tired, he looked round for a place
in which to get rest and refreshment, and soon caught
sight of a labourer's cottage.

Merlin walked in; and whether it was that his long
beard inspired respect, or whether it was that the people
of the house were nice kindly folks, it is certain that the
enchanter could not have been better received had he
been King Arthur himself. The best bread and a bowl
of new milk were placed before him, and the good
woman, in particular, seemed most anxious to please
her guest.

Merlin, however, saw that something was troubling
his hosts, and as he rested he tried to find out the cause
of their grief. The wife would not reply; but the husband, after scratching his head a long while without
finding any ideas, answered that they were sorry
because they had no children.

'If we only had a son, sir,' he went on, 'even a very
little one, no bigger than my thumb, we should be as
happy as the days are long.'

Merlin was very fond of a joke, and the idea of this great strapping ploughman having a son no bigger than his thumb amused him intensely.

'You shall have your wish, my friend,' said the magician with a smile; and after bidding them farewell he went away.

You may fancy that a man like Merlin had many friends among the fairies. Even Oberon, the Fairy King, knew him and loved him. What was of more importance in this case, Merlin was also very friendly with the Queen of the Fairies. Immediately on his return from his journey he went to her and told of his visit to the cottage and of the ploughman's strange request. Both agreed that it would be a fine jest to let the good man have exactly what he had asked for, neither more nor less.

Not a great while afterwards the ploughman's wife had a son; but you can imagine the worthy man's surprise when he first saw him, for the baby was exactly the size he had asked for – as big as his thumb! In every respect it was the prettiest little doll baby you could wish to see. The Queen of the Fairies herself came in soon after it was born, and summoned the most skilful of her followers to clothe the little stranger as a fairy child should be clothed.

A fairy verse tells us:

> An acorn hat he had for his crown;
>   His shirt it was by spiders spun;
> His coat was woven of thistle-down;
>   His trousers up with tags were done;
> His stockings, of apple-rind, they tie
> With eye-lash plucked from his mother's eye;
> His shoes were made of a mouse's skin,
> Nicely tanned, with the hair within.

Strange to say, Tom, although he grew older, as everybody has to, never grew bigger; so that the ploughman
often wished he had merely asked for a son without
saying anything about the young gentleman's size. And
he agreed with his wife in wishing he had not men-
tioned his thumb, or that Merlin had not granted his
wish so exactly to the letter; for he feared such a little
fellow would never be able to defend himself against the
rude boys of the village. But the ploughman need have
had no fears, for what Tom lacked in size he made up
for in cunning, and this made him a match for any
urchin in the place.

For instance, when he played at 'cherry-stones' with
the village boys and lost all his stones he would creep
into the bags of the winners, and steal his losings back
again. The boys could not at first understand how it was
that Tom Thumb always won, but at last he was caught
in the act, and the owner of the bag, an ugly, ill-
natured boy, cried out, 'Ah, Master Tom Thumb! I've
caught you at last! And now won't I reward you for
thieving!' Then he pulled the strings of the bag so
tightly round Tom's neck as almost to strangle him, and
gave the bag shake after shake, which knocked all the
cherry-stones against Tom's legs like so many pebbles,
and bruised him sadly. At last Tom was allowed to
come out and run home, rubbing his shins ruefully, and
promising he would 'play fair' next time. But the boys
saved him all trouble in the matter by refusing to play
with him at all.

The next scrape Tom got into was a rather serious
one. One day his mother was making a batter pudding;
and Tom, who, like a good many children, was rather
fond of putting his nose into what did not concern him,

climbed to the edge of the bowl to see if his mother mixed it properly, and to remind her, if necessary, about such little matters as putting plenty of sugar in. As he sat on the edge of the bowl his foot slipped and he went into the batter heels over head; in fact, plunged into it as boys splash into a swimming bath. The batter got into his mouth, so that he could not cry out; and he kicked and struggled so that he was soon covered with batter and quite disappeared in the thick, sticky pudding. His mother chanced to be looking round at the time, and did not see what happened. Then the pudding was tied up in a cloth and popped into the pot to boil. The water soon grew hot, and poor Tom began to kick and plunge with all his might. His mother, who had stirred him round and round, thinking that he was something in the nature of a lump of suet (for Tom, being covered with batter, could not be seen), wondered what caused the pudding to keep bumping against the top and sides of the pot, so she took off the lid to see. Greatly surprised was she to behold the pudding bobbing up and down in the pot, dancing a sort of hornpipe all by itself. She could scarcely believe her eyes, and was very much frightened. At last, deciding that the pudding must be bewitched, she determined to give it to the first person who came by.

She had not long to wait before a travelling tinker passed, crying, 'Pots and kettles to mend, oh! – pots and kettles to mend, oh!'

Tom's mother beckoned him in and gave him the pudding. The tinker, delighted to have so fine a pudding for his dinner, thanked the good woman, put it in his wallet, and trudged merrily on. But he had not gone far before he felt a funny sort of 'bump – bump – bump!'

in his wallet. At first he thought a rat had somehow got in and opened the bag to see; but, to his horror, he heard a voice from inside the pudding calling, 'Hullo! hullo! hul-l-l-o-o!' There was the pudding moving in his bag, and two little feet sticking out of it, wriggling in the funniest way possible.

At this the tinker stared till his eyes almost started from his head, for he had never seen a pudding with feet before. The voice cried, 'Let me ou-u-ut! Let me ou-u-ut!' and the pudding kicked and danced in a most alarming manner.

The tinker, greatly frightened, at once granted the request made, as he thought, by the pudding. He not only 'let' it out but 'flung' it out, right over the hedge. Then he took to his heels, and ran as hard as he could for more than a mile without once stopping to look behind. As for the pudding, it fell into a dry ditch with a great splodge, breaking into five or six pieces. Tom crept out, battered all over and battered inside.

He managed, however, to get home, crawling along like a fly that has been rescued from the cream jug. His mother was only too glad to see him; and having, after much trouble, washed the batter off, she put him to bed.

Another day Tom went with his mother to milk the cow. As it was rather windy, his mother wisely tied her little son to a thistle with a needleful of thread, lest he should be blown away. But the cow, in cropping the thistles, happened to choose the very one to which tiny Tom was tied, and gulped thistle and boy in a single mouthful. Tom, finding himself in a large red cavern, with two rows of great white 'grinders' going 'champ – champ!' cried out with fright, 'Mother! Mother!'

'Where are you, Tommy, my dear?' she cried.

The cow in cropping the thistles happened to choose the
very one to which tiny Tom was tied.

'Here, mother!' screamed Tom. 'In the brown cow's mouth!'

The mother began to weep and wring her hands, for she thought her dear little boy would be crushed into a shapeless mass; but the cow, surprised at such strange noises in her throat, opened her mouth wide and dropped Tommy on the grass. His mother was only too glad to clap him up in her apron and run home with him.

Tom was rather forward for his age, and still more so for his size, and he soon thought he ought in some way to make himself useful. To indulge the little man, his father made him a whip of a barley straw to drive the plough horses. Tom thought this very grand, and used to shout at the horses and crack his whip in fine style; but as he could never strike a horse higher than the hoof, it is doubtful whether he was of much use. One day, as he stood on a clod to aim a blow at one of the horses, his foot slipped, and he rolled over and over into a deep furrow. A raven hovering near picked up the barley-straw whip and little Tommy at one gulp. Up through the air the little man was whisked, so swiftly that it took his breath away; but presently the raven stopped to rest on the terrace of a castle belonging to a giant called Grumbo. Here the raven dropped Tom, and old Grumbo, coming soon after on the terrace for a walk, spied him perched upon a stone. Without thinking, the cruel monster snapped him up and swallowed him, clothes and all, as if he had been a pill. But Grumbo would have been wiser had he left Tom alone, for the little boy at once began to jump and dance in such a way as to make the greedy giant very uncomfortable.

Grumbo kicked and roared, and rubbed himself in the place which would have been 'under his pinny' if he had worn one; but the more he rubbed, the more Tom danced, until at last the giant became dreadfully unwell. He opened his mouth, and his inside feelings seemed to grow worse and worse, until suddenly the little passenger came flying out, right over the terrace, into the sea.

A big fish happened to be swimming by at the time, and seeing little Tom whirling through the air, took him for a kind of May fly. So he opened his mouth and swallowed. Poor Tom was now in worse plight than ever; for if he made the fish set him free, as he had made the giant, he would only have been dropped in the sea and been drowned. So his only chance was to wait patiently in the hope that the fish would be caught. It was not long before this happened; for the fish was a greedy fellow, always in search of something to eat, and never satisfied. He snapped up a bait hanging at the end of a fishing-line, and in another instant was wriggling and writhing with the hook through his gills. He was dragged up, and the fisherman, seeing what a splendid fellow he was, thought he would present him to King Arthur. So, having killed his prize, the fisherman made his way to Court, where he received a warm welcome in the royal kitchen.

The fish was much admired, and the cook took a knife and proceeded to cut it open. Great was his surprise when Master Tom popped up his head, and politely hoped that cookee was 'quite well!'

You can fancy the amazement this unexpected arrival caused. King Arthur was quickly informed that a wee knight, of extraordinary height, had come to

Court, and Master Tom met with a very hearty reception. The King made him his dwarf, and he soon became the favourite of the whole Court as the funniest, merriest little fellow they had ever seen.

In dancing Tom greatly excelled; and it became a custom with the King to place him on the table for the diversion of the company. But Tom could also run and jump with wonderful agility, and was sometimes known to leap over a thread stretched across the table at a height of $3\frac{1}{2}$ inches. Once he tried to leap over a reel of cotton that was put up on end on the table; but that was too much for him, and he fell over and hurt himself. He had at least as much cleverness in his head as in his heels, if not more. The Queen soon grew very fond of him; and as for King Arthur he scarcely ever went hunting without having Tom Thumb riding astride on his saddle-bow. If it began to rain, the little man would creep into the King's pocket, and lie there snug and warm until the shower was over; and sometimes the King would set him to ride upon his thumb, with a piece of silk cord passed through a ring for a bridle, and a whip made of a tiny stalk of grass.

One day King Arthur questioned Tom about his parentage and birth, for he was naturally curious to know where his clever little page came from.

Tom replied that his parents were poor people, and that he would be very glad of an opportunity to see them. To this the King freely consented; and that he should not go empty-handed, gave him an order on the royal treasury for as much money as he could carry. Tom made choice of a silver three-penny piece, and, having procured a little purse, with much difficulty tied it on his back. His burden made his progress very slow

The cook carried Tom on a platter to the King, but His
Majesty was fully occupied with affairs of State.

and hard, but he managed at last to reach home safely, having travelled half a mile in forty-eight hours.

There was great rejoicing on the part of his parents, for they had feared he was dead. They were especially surprised at the large sum of money he had brought. A walnut shell was placed for him by the fire-side, and his parents feasted him on a hazel-nut. But they were not so careful as they should have been, for they allowed him to eat the whole nut in three days, whereas a nut generally lasted him for a month. The consequence was that Tommy was ill and had to lie three days in the walnut-shell.

When he got well he thought it time to return to his duties at the palace; and his mother, though loth to part with him, took him in her hand, and with one puff blew him all the way to King Arthur's Court.

Here a sad disaster was in store for Tom – greater than any he had yet met. His mother had hoped he would have the good fortune that had always attended him; for indeed little Tom Thumb had gone through dangers enough to have killed three ordinary men. If she had thought of this danger she would doubtless have taken him back herself; but she trusted to chance. And indeed if the wind had been a little stronger, or a little steadier, he would have alighted quite safely; but instead of doing so, the little man came down – splash! – into a bowl of furmenty, a kind of soup of which the King was very fond, and which the royal cook was then carrying across the courtyard for the King's special enjoyment.

The splash sent the hot furmenty into the cook's eyes, and he dropped the bowl.

'Oh dear! oh dear!' he cried as he watched the rich

liquor run away and thought how angry and disappointed the King would be.

Then, to save his own skin, the artful cook pretended that Tom had played the trick on purpose to be disrespectful to His Majesty. So poor Tom was placed on trial for high treason, found guilty, and sentenced to be beheaded.

Alarmed at the cruel sentence, he looked round for a way of escape; and seeing a miller listening to the proceedings, with his mouth wide open like a great cavern, Tom, with a sudden bound, sprang down the miller's throat, unseen by all, and unknown even to the miller himself.

The prisoner having escaped, the court broke up, and the miller, who had got a touch of the hiccups, hurried home. Now Tom, having escaped from his stern judges, was equally desirous to do so from the miller's interior, which reminded him of the days when he had been swallowed by the brown cow. So, thinking the miller ought to know what was in his inside, Tom danced so many jigs and cut so many capers that the poor man, in a state of great alarm, sent messengers in every direction for medical aid; and he soon had the satisfaction of being surrounded by five learned men, among whom a fierce dispute arose as to the nature of his illness. One said that watching the mill sails turn had made him giddy; a second said that this could hardly be, for the miller was used to seeing them turn. The third declared the patient must have swallowed some water by mistake, for he certainly was not used to that, and it had disagreed. The dispute lasted so long that the miller, growing tired, gave a great yawn. Tom saw his chance and sprang out, alighting on his feet in the middle of the table. The miller, seeing who the little creature was, and remembering how he had tormented him, flew into a great rage and flung Tom out of the open window into the river.

A large salmon happened to be passing and snapped him up in a moment. Soon afterwards the salmon was caught and exposed in the market-place for sale. It was bought by the steward of a great lord; but this nobleman, thinking it a right royal fish, did not eat it himself, but sent it to King Arthur as a present. The cross old cook had the fish given to him to prepare for dinner; and when he came to cut it open, out jumped his old acquaintance, Tom Thumb. The cook was glad to be able to wreak his spite once more on his old enemy; and indeed Tom had played him too many tricks in his time, never thinking the day would come when it would be the cook's turn to play the tricks and Tommy's turn to bear them.

The cook was determined to have vengeance, so he seized poor Tom and carried him on a platter to the King, expecting that Arthur would order the culprit to be executed. But the King had no such idea, and besides, he was fully occupied with affairs of State, so he ordered the cook to bring Tom another day. The cook, although obliged to obey, was determined to serve Tom out while he could; so he shut him up in a mouse-trap for a whole week – and very miserable Tom felt. By the end of the week the King's anger was gone. He freely forgave Tom and ordered him a new suit of clothes and a good-sized mouse to ride on for a horse. Some time after he was even admitted to the honour of knighthood, and became known throughout the land as Sir Thomas Thumb.

The Queen of the Fairies climbed an almond tree covered
with blossom and sent Tom flying once more to the Court.

An old song tells what a very fine little knight he was:

> 'His shirt was made of butterflies' wings,
> His boots were made of chicken skins,
> His coat and breeches were made with pride,
> A tailor's needle hung by his side,
> A mouse for a horse he used to ride.'

The mouse-steed was a very pretty present, and little Tom rode on it, morning, noon, and night, until at last it was the means of bringing him into very great danger.

One day, when Tom was riding by a farmhouse, a large cat, seeing the mouse, rushed upon it. Tom, drawing his sword, defended himself in the bravest manner possible, and managed to keep the cat at bay until King Arthur and his knights came up. But little Sir Thomas had not passed through the combat unhurt – some of his wounds were deep and dangerous. They took him home and laid him on a bed of down on an ivory couch; but still, with all possible care and kindness, he grew worse, and it seemed that he would die. But then his old friend, the Queen of the Fairies, appeared, and bore him away to Fairyland, where she kept him for several years. Then, dressing him in bright green, she climbed an almond tree covered with blossom and sent him flying once more to the Court.

But by this time King Arthur, who had missed his little friend sadly and had often wished to have him back, was no longer there to welcome him. There had been great changes while little Sir Thomas Thumb had lived among the fairies, joining in their sports by night, and helping to make fairy rings. Good King Arthur was dead, and King Thunstone now sat on the throne.

The people flocked together from far and near to see the wonderful little hero. King Thunstone asked who he was, where he lived, and whence he came; and the little man replied:

'My name is Tom Thumb,
From the Fairies I come.
When King Arthur shone,
    This court was my home.
In me he delighted,
By him I was knighted.
Did you never hear of
    Sir Thomas Thumb?'

The King and his courtiers all smiled at the little fellow's fine verses, and the King ordered a tiny chair to be made, in order that Tom might sit on the royal table. He also caused a little palace of gold, a span high, to be built, for Tom to live in. The door was just an inch wide. Last of all, he gave him a lovely little coach to ride in, drawn by six small mice. The Queen was a rather silly woman, and because the King did not give her a new coach too, she became very jealous of Tom and told the King that he had insulted her. The King sent for him in a great rage, and to escape his fury our hero had to fly from the Court. An empty snail-shell afforded him a secure retreat for a long time, and he did not venture out till he was nearly starved.

At last the tiny fellow saw a butterfly approach his hiding-place. He sprang on its back, and it flew from flower to flower, from field to field, till at last it brought him back to King Thunstone's Court. The King, the Queen, the knights, and the cook all tried to catch the butterfly, but could not. At last poor Tom, having neither saddle nor bridle, slipped from his seat and fell into a water-can, where he was nearly drowned. The Queen vowed he should still be beheaded, and he was put back into the mouse-trap. But that night, a cat, seeing something move and supposing it to be a mouse, patted the trap about until she broke it, and Tom was able to make another dash for freedom.

The Queen, thinking that he bore a charmed life, and must therefore be a special favourite of the fairies, at last forgave him, and he was reinstated in royal favour. After that he lived for several years, having many more wonderful adventures and fights with animals of various kinds. But we must hasten on to the last sad scene of his life, and tell how poor little Tom came by his death.

One day he was walking through the palace garden, not thinking of danger, when he felt himself seized from behind by two skinny arms, and a puff of poisonous breath came in his face: he turned round and drew his sword, and for the next quarter of an hour fought valiantly against a great spider, who had mistaken him for a fly. At last the spider, having had five of his legs cut off, turned on his back, kicked out as well as he could with the remainder, and – died! Tom was victor, but his victory had been dearly bought. The spider's poisonous breath had been too much for our brave little hero, and he fell into a wasting sickness and died.

Puss in Boots

THERE was once an old miller who had three sons. When he knew that he was about to die he called his sons to the bedside and divided his property among them. This was not very difficult in one way, because he had only three possessions, his mill, his ass, and his cat, and yet no one could say that the division he made was quite fair.

The eldest son had the mill. He was well off enough, for the farmers and neighbours would give him plenty of work; and with industry and honesty he could look to becoming a rich man.

The second son, though not so lucky, had a useful, steady servant, but it was hard to see how he could depend on the ass for his living. An ass is very well as far as it goes; the difficulty is to make it go far enough. The miller's second son had, however, some hopes of getting employment from his brother, who would require a beast of burden to carry the sacks of corn to the mill and then to take the sacks of flour back to the customers.

But the third son was in a sorry plight, and really it did not seem that the miller had been fair to him. True, it was a fine cat, with thick fur and a handsome tail, but, after all, a cat is only a cat! So the poor man sat down and wondered what he should do for a living; and the more he wondered the less able was he to come to a decision.

At last he began to bemoan aloud. 'My brothers,' he said, 'by putting their property together and helping each other may do very well. There is always corn to be ground, and either sacks to be carried or odd jobs that an ass can do. As for me, so far as I can see, when I have killed my cat, and made a fur cap or a pair of mittens of his skin, I shall have disposed of all my property, and must die of hunger.'

The cat had been listening to every word his master said, and when he paused in his complainings, he came forward, and in a clear voice said, 'Dear master, do not be so troubled. You had better not kill me; I shall be far more useful to you alive than dead.'

'How can that be?' asked the young man, much surprised to find that he possessed a cat that could talk.

'If you will only give me a pair of boots and a sack,' said Puss, 'you shall have no cause for complaint.'

The young man did not quite see how this would better his condition. However, he was so poor that he could hardly be worse off, and as the cat had always been very clever in catching rats and mice, he thought it best to see what Puss would do for him.

A bootmaker was sent for, and the miller's son managed to persuade him to hold over his bill until Puss had brought in the promised fortune. The bootmaker took the measures very carefully, and when the boots came home the cat drew them on as if he had been used to such things all his life. And very nice boots they were too, for the bootmaker had worked with a will and done his very best. The sack was easily secured from the mill, and this, too, met with Pussy's approval.

The next morning the cat rose with the sun, licked himself carefully all over, trimmed his whiskers, pulled on his fine new boots, hung the sack round his neck, and then crept to a rabbit-warren, taking care to keep out of sight of the bunnies. Here he opened his sack, into which he had put some bran and lettuce leaves, and, with the loose strings in his hand, stretched himself out under a bush and pretended to be asleep.

He had not long to wait. There are plenty of foolish young rabbits in every warren, and presently a couple of giddy bunnies came hopping up, twitching their long ears. After sniffing at the opening of the sack for a moment or so, they hopped gaily in and began munching and nibbling the lettuce leaves as hard as they could, little thinking, poor simple things, of the fate that awaited them.

Master Puss had been watching with the mouth of of the sack wide open, and his paws well on the string, ready to pull at the right moment.

Whisk! – the cat pulled the string, the sack closed, and the poor bunnies inside kicked frantically to be let out. Master Puss lost no time in killing them, and, slinging the sack over his shoulder, set off to the palace, telling the guard at the gate that he wished to speak to the King.

Puss looked so fierce and determined as he twirled his whiskers that the sentries let him pass without demur. He walked straight into the King's private room, and bowing gracefully and waving his tail, said:

'My master, the Lord Marquis of Carabas' – (this title was out of the cat's own head) – 'presents his most

M.W. Tarrant

When the boots came home Puss drew them on as if he had
been used to such things all his life.

dutiful respects to your Majesty, and has commanded me to offer his humble duty, and to assure your Majesty that among your subjects none is more devoted than my master.' Here the cat made a very low bow, and the King wondered what was coming next.

The cat continued, 'My master, the Lord Marquis of Carabas, humbly sends this small present of game for the gracious acceptance of your Majesty, as a slight token of the overflowing sense of affectionate veneration with which your Majesty has inspired him.'

There was a speech for a cat to make!

The King, who was not so eloquent as his visitor, could not help feeling impressed by the beautiful long words the cat used. He had never heard of the Marquis of Carabas, but being polite – as all kings learn to be – he did not like to say so and answered graciously, 'Tell my Lord Marquis that I accept his present with great pleasure, and am much obliged to him.'

At the same time he could not help wondering how it was that he had never heard of the Marquis before. But Pussy's face wore such a look of sincerity that not the slightest shadow of suspicion that he was being imposed upon entered his kingly mind; and certainly the fine airs and manner of speech of the cat seemed to show that he belonged to a master of high degree.

All this was certainly very clever of the cat; but it was only the beginning of what he meant to do to make his master's fortune.

Bowing again to the King and flourishing his tail, he retired with all the grace and air of a thorough-bred courtier.

A day or two afterwards, Puss went again with his boots and his sack to try his fortune in the chase. This time a couple of young partridges, unused to the world and its ways, poked their beaks into the trap, and were quickly bagged and killed. These the cat also presented to the King as coming from the Lord Marquis of Carabas; and the speech he made was so eloquent, and had so many long words in it, that we had better not attempt to write it down but must leave you to imagine its beauty.

For some time the cat continued to bring a present of game to the King every day or two. His Majesty was so pleased that he gave orders that Puss should be taken down to the kitchen and given something to eat and drink whenever he called. While enjoying this good fare the faithful creature would contrive to speak to the royal servants of the large preserves and abundant game which belonged to his noble master.

Hearing one day that the King and his lovely daughter were going to take a drive by the river-side, Puss concocted a very clever scheme.

Rushing into his master's presence, he said, 'Go and bathe in the river, dear master, and I will make your fortune for you. Only bathe in the river, and leave the rest to me.'

The so-called Marquis did not see how he was to make his fortune by bathing; but by this time he was so impressed by the cat's cleverness that he would have done anything Puss told him. As he was bathing, the King drove by with his daughter, the loveliest and most beautiful Princess in the world.

As soon as the royal carriage came in sight, Puss began to run to and fro, wringing his paws and tossing them wildly over his head, while he cried at the top of his voice:

'Help! Help! Help! My Lord Marquis of Carabas is drowning! Come and h-e-l-p my Lord – Marquis – of – Ca-ra-ba-a-as!'

Hearing this pitiful wail, the King looked out of the carriage window; and, recognizing the cat who had brought him so many presents of game and made such beautiful speeches, he at once ordered his guards to go to the assistance of the Lord Marquis.

But this was only the beginning of the cat's scheme. Knowing that his master's shabby clothes would never do for a Marquis, he had hidden them under a big stone. He now ran to the carriage window and said to his Majesty:

'My Lord Marquis's clothes have been stolen while he was bathing, and the Marquis is shivering very much, with nothing to put on. He would like to wait upon your Majesty and the illustrious Princess, but of course he cannot do so without clothes.'

'Oh,' said the King with a laugh, 'we'll soon remedy that.' He thereupon ordered a suit from his own wardrobe to be brought for the Marquis.

It is an old saying that fine feathers make fine birds; and the young miller certainly looked very well indeed in his new garments, as he came up to the carriage to thank the King for his kindness. His Majesty was so taken with him that he insisted that my Lord Marquis should come into the carriage and drive with them; and the beautiful Princess looked as if she were not at all displeased with the proposal.

The young man felt rather bashful in his new position. But this was perhaps to his advantage; for the old King thought he was silent out of gratitude at the honour of being asked to ride in the King's carriage, while the lovely daughter for her part had no doubt the Marquis was speechless with admiration of her beauty. The King told a number of very long stories as they rode along; and as the Marquis said, 'Yes, your Majesty' to everything, and seemed much interested, the King was perfectly satisfied, and thought him a well-informed and modest young man. The fact was, the Marquis was thinking all the time of the scrape he had got into, and wondering what the King and his lovely daughter would say to that rogue Puss if they only knew how he had imposed on them.

But Puss was not the cat to leave his master in the lurch. He knew that people judged by appearances; and he had determined that his master should appear a wealthy man.

As soon as he had seen the young man safely seated in the King's carriage, he struck across the fields by a short cut and soon got a long way in advance of the royal party. In a wheat-field a party of reapers were gathering in the harvest. The cat ran up to them, and doubling up his paws in a most expressive manner, said:

'Now, good people, if you don't say, when the King asks, that this field belongs to the Lord Marquis of Carabas, you will all be chopped up into mincemeat.'

The reapers, startled by the appearance of the fierce little booted creature, promised at once to do as they were told.

Soon afterwards the royal carriage passed, and the King stopped, as the cat had supposed he would. Beckoning one of the reapers, the King asked to whom all that fine wheat belonged.

The good people, remembering the threats Puss had made, replied:

The Ogre himself came to the door, carrying his great
spiked club.

'To the Marquis of Carabas, your Majesty.'

'You have a fine crop of wheat, my Lord Marquis,' said the King; 'I am rather a judge of wheat.'

'Yes, your Majesty,' replied the Marquis; and the King thought again what a nice young man he was.

Meanwhile the cat came to a meadow where the mowers with their scythes were cutting the long grass.

'Good people,' said Master Puss, running up. 'When the King asks you presently to whom this meadow belongs, if you do not say "To the Marquis of Carabas," you will all be chopped up into mincemeat.'

When the King passed he did not fail to ask to whom the fields belonged, and was much surprised at being answered again, 'To the Marquis of Carabas, your Majesty.'

'Really, my Lord Marquis, your possessions are very great!' said the King; whereat the young man blushed and answered, 'Yes, your Majesty.' And now the Princess thought he looked handsomer than ever. In fact, she was fast falling in love with him.

As they drove on the cat always ran before, saying the same thing to everybody he came across – that they were to declare the whole country belonged to his master.

But though the Marquis had no castle, there was a personage in those parts who had – and a fine castle it was. This personage was an Ogre, a giant, and a magician, all in one. The cat knew all about him and his wicked ways. Going boldly to the door, he rang a loud peal at the bell, and called out to the Ogre that he had come to pay a friendly visit and to inquire after his welfare. The cat did not really care about the giant's well-being; but the giant was the owner of much land,

in fact, of those very fields and meadows which the cat
had persuaded the workers to describe as belonging to
the Marquis of Carabas. The Ogre himself came to the
door, carrying his great spiked club. Bowing low, and
doffing his plumed hat, Puss repeated his words and
said he trusted the Ogre was now better. (The fact was,
the Ogre had eaten a huntsman, top-boots and all, a
few weeks before, and the spurs had disagreed with
him.)

The Ogre replied that he was much obliged to the cat
for his politeness, and invited him to walk inside. This
was just what the cat wanted. He at once accepted the
invitation, and, sitting on a table, began to talk to his
host in his politest manner.

'Sir,' he began, 'everyone says you are a very clever
magician.'

'That is true,' answered the Ogre, who was very vain.

'Sir,' continued the cat, 'I have heard that you are
able to transform yourself into the shape of various
animals.'

'That also is true,' answered the Ogre.

'But, sir,' continued the cunning cat, 'I mean large
animals, such, for instance, as an elephant.'

'Quite true,' answered the Ogre. 'See for yourself.'

He muttered some magical words, and stood before
the cat in the shape of an elephant, with large flapping
ears, sharp tusks, little eyes, and long trunk – all com-
plete.

The cat was startled at this sudden change; but,
mustering courage, went on: 'Well, sir, that is marvel-
lous indeed! But can you change your shape at will, and
represent whatever animal you choose?'

The Ogre wondered somewhat to find the cat so

anxious to obtain useful knowledge. But most people are flattered at being thought clever and like to exhibit their talents. So the Ogre resolved to gratify the curiosity of Puss.

The elephant waved his trunk three times in the air, and then stood before the astonished cat in the shape of a huge African lion, with waving mane, a huge head, and the most awful set of big white teeth. The cat stood gazing at him like a creature transfixed with fright, just as he, in his time, had seen many a poor mouse terrified and trembling, and unable from very fear to fly from danger.

When the lion opened his mouth and gave a roar, the cat was so awestruck that he dashed straight up the wall, and, reaching a window, escaped on to the roof of the castle. His polished boots were very much in the way, but terror lent him wings, or rather feet, and his boots scarcely received a moment's thought. There he stood on the roof, quaking, and yet spitting and snarling, as it is cat nature to do, while every hair on his tail rose on end with horror. He could hear the Ogre below laughing at the thought of how he had frightened his visitor.

But presently Puss recovered courage, for he was a very brave cat, and felt ashamed of himself for having been so easily frightened. He knew by the laugh that the Ogre had now resumed his natural shape, so he came down again into the room with a cool and collected air, muttering something about the heat of the room, which had compelled him to run out for a breath of fresh air. At this the Ogre laughed louder than ever, but the cat sat down again on the table, and resumed the conversation as if nothing had happened.

'Sir,' he went on, 'I should not have believed these wonders if I had not seen them with my own eyes. You are the greatest magician it has ever been my good fortune to meet.'

The Ogre made a deep bow and seemed much gratified.

'I have long heard of your fame and skill, but what I have seen far surpasses all my ideas of what a magician could achieve.'

Here the Ogre again bent forward and made a deep bow. He was beginning to think the cat really had a good deal of sense after all.

'But once,' went on Puss, 'I heard of a conjuror who could not only assume the shape of a large animal like an elephant or a lion, but that of the smallest also – for instance, he would appear as a rat or a mouse. But then, you know, he was an old magician, who had been practising for a great number of years, and I do not expect that I shall ever find anyone who could quite come up to him.'

'Don't you, indeed!' cried the Ogre angrily. 'You fancy he was a greater man than I? Ha! ha! – I'll show you that I can do the same thing.'

In a second or two the Ogre was capering about the room in the shape of a little mouse. This was exactly what the cat wanted.

He instantly sprung on the mouse, and a single nip with his sharp teeth put an end to the Ogre.

The cat, cunning fellow, had now gained his object. Here was a castle for the Marquis of Carabas – a sumptuous mansion in which no King need be ashamed to rest after a long ride; and the cat thought, with glee, how surprised the Marquis would be on his arrival.

Sure enough, just as Puss sat slyly licking his lips after swallowing the Ogre, the King's carriage came in sight.

The cat had only just time to run upstairs and dress in a page's doublet when the King's coach appeared in front of the castle.

There, to the great surprise of the Marquis of Carabas, stood Puss, gallantly attired, and looking as much at his ease as if he had done nothing but look after the castle all his life. Not only did his clothes give him a very dignified air, but he wore them with a grace which greatly increased their effect; and nothing could exceed the courtly air with which he welcomed the King and Princess to the castle.

'Welcome, your Majesty and your Royal Highness,' he said, bowing low, 'to the poor castle of my master, the Lord Marquis of Carabas! If your Majesty and the gracious Princess will be pleased to alight and take some refreshment, this will indeed be the proudest day of my life, and of my master's, the Lord Marquis of Carabas.'

He made another deep bow, waved his cap, and laid his paw upon his heart.

'Upon our royal word, my Lord Marquis,' cried the King, 'you have a splendid castle, and we shall have great pleasure in viewing it more closely. We are always happy to visit our loving subjects; and, moreover, shall be glad to stretch our royal legs; also our long ride has given us an appetite.' (The King said this as a hint that some luncheon would be acceptable, and the sly cat took the hint, as you will see.) 'What say you, daughter? Will you be of the party?'

The Princess, whose curiosity had been raised by the aspect of the castle, was quite willing; and the King commanded the Marquis to give the Princess his hand and conduct her into his dwelling.

Puss led the way, walking backwards and bowing with the grace and ease of a lord chamberlain.

The castle was splendidly furnished, for the Ogre had been a person of taste. Every room was hung with costly tapestry, and in the stables were a number of fine horses and a grand gilded coach in which the King himself would not have disdained to ride. Indeed, the Princess, after looking at it attentively and trying the cushions, went so far as to remark smilingly that it was very comfortable and that it seemed fit for a married couple; whereat the cat nudged his master to make a bow.

While they were walking through the upper rooms, the cat slipped away for a few minutes to the kitchen. Here he looked quickly into the various cupboards and was delighted to find everything he wanted – rich meats, and salads, fruits, ices and sweets, and the choicest of wines.

When the royal party returned to the great hall – lo and behold! – he had spread a luncheon such as any King and Princess might have been glad to sit down to.

The Marquis invited the King to be seated, and himself handed the Princess to a chair. If the King had been good-humoured before, he was radiant now; for he was rather fond of his meals, and the luncheon was faultless, the Ogre having made a point of having the best of everything.

With each glass of wine the King became more jovial, and appeared to conceive a greater affection for the Marquis. At last he began to treat him almost as a father might a son, and after luncheon he said:

'It will be your own fault, my Lord of Carabas, if you

do not become our son-in-law, provided, of course, our daughter has no objection.'

At this plain speech the young lady became scarlet with confusion, but she made no objection and did not look displeased. Indeed, she had long ago made up her mind that the Marquis was the handsomest and most attractive young man she had ever met, and you may be sure, being a Princess, she had met many.

So the Marquis of Carabas made a little speech (not nearly so fine as the cat could have made it for him), in which he thanked the King for his condescension, and expressed himself still more glad that the Princess had been graciously pleased to offer no objection; and as it was generally supposed that silence gave consent, he supposed it to be the case with this honour, and he accepted it accordingly.

As for the cat, he was obliged to go into the courtyard to hide his joy, which was so great that he stood on his head on the flagstones and kicked his hind legs in the air.

Little more remains to be told. The Marquis returned with the King and the Princess to the royal palace; and the marriage took place a few days later amid great rejoicings.

The Marquis of Carabas made a good and kind husband, and neither he nor the Princess had cause to regret what had happened. As for the cat, he was made a great lord, and never had occasion to run after mice except for his own amusement.

The marriage of the Marquis and the Princess took place
a few days later.

Beauty and the Beast

IN a large city of the East once lived a very rich merchant, who had a splendid house and large warehouses full of costly goods; a hundred guests sat down at his table every day.

His family consisted of three sons and three daughters. The sons were tall, well-grown young men, and the daughters were all very handsome, especially the youngest. So bright and happy was her face, and so winning were her ways, that, as a child, she had been the pet of the family, and everyone had called her 'Little Beauty'. Now that she was a tall, grown-up girl, the name still clung to her, and this made her sisters very jealous.

The youngest daughter was not only better-looking than her sisters but better-tempered. The sisters were very vain of their wealth and position, gave themselves many airs, and declined to visit the daughters of other merchants on the ground that only persons of quality were fit to speak to them. Every day they went to balls, plays and parties, and made fun of Little Beauty for preferring to spend her time in reading and other useful occupations. As their father was known to be so wealthy, the two elder sisters received many offers of marriage, but they always declared that they would accept no one below the rank of duke or earl. Beauty also had many offers, though she said less about them, and always told her lovers that she thought she was too young to marry and would rather spend some years longer with her father, whom she dearly loved.

Happy indeed was it for the merchant that he loved his sons and daughters better than his wealth; for he little thought, as he sat at the head of his plentifully supplied table, with his smiling guests around him, that several terrible misfortunes had happened, and that he was, in fact, no better than a ruined man. One of his largest ships, with a very costly cargo, was wrecked at sea, and only two of the sailors were saved, after clinging for days to the fragment of a mast; another equally valuable vessel was taken by pirates; and a third fell into the hands of the enemy's fleet. By land he was equally unfortunate: his largest warehouse was burned, and robbers attacked and plundered a caravan conveying his goods across the desert. So, within a few months, he sank from the height of wealth to the depth of poverty and want.

Very different from their former splendid mansion was the quiet little country cottage to which the merchant and his family now removed. There were no pleasure-grounds, fountains, groves of trees, or ornamental waters. The once wealthy merchant, who had employed hundreds of servants, was now reduced to toil in the fields with his sons to gain a bare living; and they had to work early and late to procure even that. Hard as their lot seemed, the three sons manfully met the reverses of fortune, and both by word and deed did all in their power to help their father.

The two elder daughters were far different, for they spent all their time fretting over their losses, and their grumbling not only rendered privation doubly hard for themselves but embittered the lot of the merchant and his sons. They would not enjoy the plain fare the others ate with relish; they rose late, and spent the days in idleness, too proud and lazy to devote themselves to any useful task, and despising their brothers for working hard.

While her two elder sisters sat crying and sobbing, Beauty would be fully employed in spinning or in seeing to the household affairs; and she always had a smile for her father and her brothers when they came in wearied from their work.

By working hard, morning, noon, and night, the merchant and his sons were fortunate to earn enough to keep them from want. In fact, in one respect the merchant was better off, for whereas, during the time of his prosperity, he had often been kept awake at night by anxious thoughts for the safety of his ships, his warehouses, and his stores of gold and silver, such thoughts now never entered his mind, and he slept soundly and peacefully till morning. Also his conscience was clear, for he had always been honourable in his dealings, and, though everyone knew of his misfortunes, he was still respected by all whose respect was worth having.

After they had lived in this way for about a year a great change came over their quiet life. One day a messenger arrived at the merchant's cottage with an important letter. It contained news that a ship, long given up as wrecked and lost, had safely anchored in a distant port, and the merchant was desired to go and take possession without the loss of a day.

You can fancy what a stir this made in the little household. The merchant's sons looked hopeful, and the two elder sisters, radiant with smiles, began at once to discuss plans for future pleasures. Beauty was glad too; but she was chiefly glad because she loved to see her father happy. The merchant was pleased at the prospect of regaining a portion of his wealth more for his children's sake than for his own, and he had a hundred projects for giving his daughters handsome presents on his return.

Before he started, he asked each in turn what special present she would like him to bring home when he had received the money for his cargo. The two elder sisters, who had counted on this very question, were at once ready with a long list of things they wanted, chiefly fine dresses and jewels; and their requests somewhat surprised and pained their father, for they seemed to think his whole fortune had been restored instead of a single vessel.

He, however, promised that they should have what they wanted if he could possibly secure it. Beauty had not been thinking about herself at all, and when she heard what her sisters wanted decided that all the ship contained would not suffice to cover the cost.

'Well, Beauty,' asked her father, 'and what do you desire? What can I bring you, my child?'

'Nothing at all, thank you, father,' she replied.

But when he seemed hurt at this she kissed him and flung her arms round his neck, saying:

'Yes, dear father, there is one thing I should love. We have no flowers in our little garden here, though I am sure it is very nice. Please bring me, if you can, a single red rose.'

Beauty, indeed, had never cared for wealth, and only made this request so that she might not seem to be affronting her greedy sisters.

The sisters laughed at Beauty in secret for what they called her stupid choice; but did not dare to say so openly, for fear of their brothers.

The merchant rode off on a horse he had borrowed from a friend, the three daughters standing at the door, waving their handkerchiefs, and crying 'Good-bye!' But it was Beauty who got the last kiss.

The merchant's journey was not so prosperous as he had hoped. The cargo, indeed, had been saved, and the ship was safe in port; but a lawsuit had ensued, and there was so much to pay that the merchant set out for home not much richer than he had left it. On his return he met with a wonderful adventure, which was to have some strange results.

Night had fallen as he was riding through a thick wood, and he lost his way, though he fancied he could not be far from home. His weary horse still carried him on, and he looked anxiously round for some building where he could find shelter until morning; for the rain was beating down and the wolves howled in the darkness round about.

All at once he became aware of a long avenue of trees, at the end of which a light glimmered. This proved to be a lamp, hung at the entrance to a large and splendid palace.

WELCOME, WEARY TRAVELLER

was written in Eastern characters over the heavy, massive gate of iron. This gate appeared to be closed; but at the traveller's approach, to his great amazement, it swung slowly back on its hinges, though no porter appeared to open it. The message over the gate emboldened the wayfarer to ride into the courtyard; and an inner door, also opening of itself, disclosed a large stable, with room for fifty horses, but quite empty.

The merchant put up his weary horse, fed him on the oats and hay he saw ready to hand, and then went to try and find someone in the palace. In the vestibule was a fountain which sent up a sparkling jet from a marble basin, and gave a delicious air of coolness to all around. From this he went on through many large apartments, all splendidly furnished, but with no one in them – not even a servant to take care of the house. In one of the rooms a fire was burning, and here was a table containing some very tempting dishes, though there was only one plate and a single knife and fork. After waiting in doubt for some time, hoping the owner of the house would appear, the hungry merchant sat down and made a hearty meal, drinking his own health afterwards.

As it was now time to rest, the merchant went upstairs. On the upper floor were several bedrooms, with large beds and handsome furniture. In one the merchant determined to pass the night, rightly thinking that the welcome to travellers inscribed over the gateway must include a bed upon which to repose. Still, he was puzzled that with all the order and neatness visible throughout the palace, no living being appeared to whom he could speak. But he was too tired to think very much about it, and soon fell fast asleep.

When he awoke the next morning, greatly refreshed, he was amazed to see that a new suit of clothes had been placed ready for him to put on instead of his own, which were torn and travel-stained.

'Surely,' he thought, 'this place must belong to some kind fairy who has taken pity on my ill-luck.'

He then went downstairs to the room where he had supped, and was pleased, though not altogether surprised, to find the breakfast-table ready prepared, with everything he could wish to eat and drink.

Seeing that a door leading to a beautiful garden stood open, he put on his hat, hoping that he might meet his kind host and have an opportunity of thanking him.

In the garden also everything was in first-rate order. The flower-beds were full of beautiful plants, the walks clean and hard, the grass-plots soft and smooth as velvet carpets.

At the end of one path stood a lovely arbour, shaded by a splendid rose tree in full bloom. This set the merchant thinking of his daughter Beauty's wish for a red rose; he selected the very best he could find and plucked it. A moment later came a tremendous roar, like that of an angry lion disturbed by a hunter. In terror, he fell on his knees and covered his face with his hands, dreading to look up, lest he should see some wild beast ready to spring upon him. Then he heard another great roar, and a heavy hand was laid on his shoulder: he rose and saw a monster with a beast's head but of the shape of a man, covered with fur. The creature stood glaring at him in a threatening manner, and then said, in a terrible voice, 'Ungrateful man! I saved your life by admitting you into my palace. I gave you rest and refreshment and clothes, and you requite my kindness by stealing the only thing I prize – my beautiful roses. For this you shall surely atone. Prepare for death!'

The merchant, in utter terror, again fell on his knees and begged for forgiveness, calling the Beast 'my lord',

Directly he had plucked the rose the merchant saw a
monster with a beast's head but of the shape of a man, who
stood glaring at him in a threatening manner.

and declaring that he meant no harm, but had only plucked the rose for his youngest daughter, whom he loved, and who had wished for one.

'I will spare no one who steals my roses,' roared the Beast, 'whatever excuse he makes.'

The merchant again pleaded for his life, telling how his daughter, Beauty, had asked for nothing but a single rose, while her sisters had desired jewels and gay apparel. At last, by dint of entreaty, he prevailed.

'You shall have your life on one condition,' replied the Beast. 'You have told me this story of your daughters, but how am I to know that it is true? I will spare your life and allow you to go home only if you promise to bring one of them to suffer in your stead. If she refuses to come, you must promise faithfully to be back yourself within three months. And don't call me "my lord", for I hate flattery; I am not a lord, but a Beast! Promise, or die! And choose quickly!'

The merchant, who was very tender-hearted, had not the least intention of letting one of his daughters die for his sake; but he thought it best to agree to the Beast's conditions, for he would at least have the satisfaction of seeing his family again. So he gave his promise and turned sorrowfully away.

'Go to the room you slept in,' cried the Beast after him. 'You may fill a chest with gold and jewels or whatsoever you like best to take home with you, but woe betide you if you are not back on the appointed day.'

When he reached the room the merchant, reflecting that he must in any case die – for, being an upright and honourable man, he had no thought of breaking a promise made even to a Beast – decided that he might as well have the comfort of leaving his children well provided for, especially as there were heaps of gold pieces lying about. He accordingly filled the chest with gold and departed, leaving the palace as sorrowful as he had been glad when he first beheld it.

When he reached his own house, his daughters warmly welcomed him, but were struck with the settled sadness in his face. In silence he gave the elder sisters the costly presents he had brought for them, and then sat down, evidently still very troubled. Beauty ran at once and threw her arms round his neck to comfort him.

'Ah, my dear Beauty, here is your red rose,' said the merchant; 'but you little know the price your poor father has promised to pay for it.' And he told her everything that had occurred.

The elder sisters left off examining their presents and came up to listen. When they understood the cause of their father's sadness, they began to throw all the blame on poor Beauty. 'If the affected little thing had only asked for presents like ours,' they declared, 'this trouble would not have come, and our dear father would not be in danger of his life. She pretends to be so much better than other people, but though she will be the cause of her father's death she does not shed a single tear.'

'It would be quite useless to do so,' said Beauty quietly, 'for my father will not die. As the Beast said he would accept one of the daughters, I am going to give myself up to him, and so prove my love for the best of fathers.'

The brothers would not hear of this and begged hard to be allowed to go and kill the monster. The father, however, was firm to his pledge, and knew that the Beast would not be put off. He had also secret hopes that Beauty's life would after all be spared; for the

Beast's generosity had made him think that, as he had so far relented as to send him away with piles of gold, his intentions might not be so murderous as his words. He also hoped that the appearance of Beauty and her charming manners would produce an effect, as they had always done in her own home; and that the monster would not really care to take the life of so young and innocent a creature.

The sisters secretly exulted at Beauty's sad fate, for they had always been jealous of her, because she was the favourite of their father. But the brothers were really and truly grieved, and kissed their sister heartily when the three months had expired, and the time had come for her to set out with her father on their sorrowful journey.

The domain around the Beast's castle was very beautiful. Birds with splendid plumage flew about, singing merry songs as they built their nests in the thick trees. In spite of the sorrowful nature of their errand, the two travellers could not help feeling a little comforted by the beauty of the scene; and the nearer they came to the Beast's palace, the fresher became the greenery, and the thicker the throng of chirping birds.

In due time they reached the palace, which they found deserted, as on the merchant's first visit. The horse, without bidding, went into the same stable as before. In the spacious reception-hall they found a magnificent supper laid, with covers for two persons. There was every imaginable dainty on the table, but Beauty could hardly eat a mite for terror, while her father was overwhelmed with fear of what was to come. He had seen the terrible Beast, and knew what a large mouth and ugly fangs he had, and how, in every respect, he was just the sort of creature to frighten Beauty out of her wits, and he dreaded what might be the effect of the Beast's appearance.

When supper was over, a heavy tread sounded along the corridor; the door of the room was thrown open, and the Beast stalked in. And, oh! he was far, far uglier than Beauty imagined he possibly could be! And he had *such* a mouth, and two such ugly teeth came right over his lower jaw!

Beauty did her best to hide her fear. The creature walked right up to her, eyed her all over, and then asked in a gruff voice:

'Have you come here of your own free will?'

'Yes,' she faltered out.

The monster then said in a softened tone, 'You are a good girl. I am much obliged to you.'

This mild behaviour somewhat raised the hopes of the merchant; but they were instantly damped by the Beast's turning towards him, and gruffly commanding him to quit the castle and never return again under pain of death. Having given this order in a tone which showed he intended to be obeyed, the Beast retired with a bow and a good-night to Beauty, and a glance at her father which seemed to say, 'Make haste off.'

'Ah, my dear Beauty,' said the merchant, kissing his daughter tenderly, 'I am half dead already at the thought of leaving you at the mercy of this dreadful Beast. You shall go back home and leave me here.'

'No, indeed,' said Beauty boldly, 'I will never agree to that. You must go at once, or the Beast will certainly kill you.'

At length the merchant departed, after kissing his daughter again a score of times, while she, poor girl, tried to raise his spirits by feigning a courage she was far from feeling. When he had gone, she took a candle-stick and wandered along the corridor in search of her room: soon she came to a door on which was inscribed in large letters:

BEAUTY'S ROOM.

She timidly opened the door and found herself in a large room, beautifully furnished, with book-cases, sofas, pictures, and a guitar and other musical instruments.

'The Beast does not mean to eat me up at once,' she thought, 'or he would never have taken all this trouble.'

So, a little comforted, she retired to rest, and, ex-hausted with her journey and her fears, quickly fell asleep.

Next morning she examined her room more closely. On the first leaf of an album was written her own name – BEAUTY; and beneath it, in letters of gold, she read the following verse:

'Beauteous lady, dry your tears;
Here's no cause for sighs or fears:
Command as freely as you may,
For you command and I obey.'

This was a very comforting verse indeed, but Beauty still felt very unhappy, very lonely, and very anxious to know what was to befall her.

'Ah!' sighed the poor girl, 'if I might have a wish granted, it would be to see my poor father and what he is doing.'

She turned as she spoke and, to her great surprise, saw in a mirror opposite a picture of her home. The merchant, distracted with grief, was lying on a couch; and her two sisters were at the window, looking listlessly out. At this sight poor Beauty wept bitterly; but after a time she regained her fortitude, and went down to the dining-hall. She wondered not a little to see the hall still quite empty. Not a person appeared to welcome her, but a dainty meal had been spread, as on the previous day. But at supper, as she was about to seat herself at table, the Beast came in and humbly requested permission to stay and see her eat.

Beauty, who somehow now did not feel nearly so much afraid of him and was utterly tired of being alone, replied, 'Yes, if you wish to do so.'

All the while she was eating the Beast sat by, looking at her very respectfully but with great admiration. He soon began to talk, and astonished her by his wit and the extent of his knowledge on various subjects. At last he leaned over the table and, peering intently at her face, asked suddenly:

'Do you think me so very, very ugly?'

Beauty was obliged to reply, 'Yes, shockingly ugly!' but, fearing to hurt his feelings, added that he could not help his looks.

This did not seem to console the poor Beast much, for he sighed deeply. After sitting a while in silence, he seemed to collect all his courage for one grand effort and asked Beauty – to her great astonishment – 'Will you marry me?'

'No, Beast,' she replied at once in a very decided way; whereupon her suitor gave a great sigh which nearly blew out the candles, and retired, looking very doleful.

For some little time Beauty's life was a very quiet one. She roamed about the palace and through the gardens just as she pleased, invisible attendants bringing her whatever she wished for. Each evening the Beast would come to supper, and try to entertain her as best he

Every evening at supper he would ask the old question,
'Beauty, will you marry me?'

could; and he was so well-informed and talked so sensibly that Beauty began to like him. Still, his hideous form shocked her each time she looked at him; and whenever her host, after doing his utmost to be agreeable all the evening, repeated his question, 'Will you marry me, Beauty?' she always gave a very decided refusal in the unmistakable words, 'No, Beast.'

Then the Beast would give one of his tremendous sighs and retire; but the next evening he was always there again, and when he asked the old question, 'Beauty, will you marry me?' she always replied, 'No, Beast.'

But soon Beauty began to be homesick; the more so, as her magic mirror, which she never failed to consult each day, showed that her father was pining for her very much. His sons had gone to fight their country's battles, and his two eldest daughters had got married and were constantly quarrelling with their husbands. So, you see, the merchant was rather dull and lonely.

At last Beauty summoned up courage to beg the Beast to let her go home and see her father. He was at first much alarmed at the proposal, fearing she might forget to come back again; but at last he consented, after exacting a promise that she would not be away long.

He spoke very kindly to her on the matter, and indeed always treated her with great kindness and courtesy, though she had so frequently refused to marry him.

'Tomorrow morning,' said the Beast, 'you will find yourself at your father's house. But pray, pray do not forget me in my loneliness. When you are ready to come back, you have only to lay the ring I here give you on your dressing-table before you lie down at night.'

Beauty took the ring, and the Beast bade her a sorrowful farewell.

Beauty retired to rest; and, sure enough, when she awoke in the morning, she was in her old bed at her father's house. By the glimmering light of dawn, she could see that nothing in the room had changed. It was all kept, by her father's directions, just as she had left it. But one thing surprised and pleased her greatly, for which she could not in any way account. By the bedside lay a large chest full of beautiful apparel and costly jewels.

You may fancy how glad her father was to see her. But the envious sisters, who were there on a visit, were not at all pleased. When they saw the chest they at once declared that the presents must have been intended by the Beast for them; whereupon the box disappeared, as a gentle hint that they were mistaken.

On the failure of this selfish scheme, they resolved, as they termed it, 'to serve her out' by making her stay too long, hoping the Beast would be very angry, and punish her accordingly. The days passed happily away; and the sisters behaved with such false kindness that Beauty was prevailed upon to stay – first one excuse was made to prevent her going, and then another. This day a friend was coming who would be disappointed if he did not find her; the next they themselves could not make up their minds to part with their darling sister. So the days glided by, and Beauty prolonged her visit, first for one week, and then two weeks, longer than she had intended to stay.

But what was the Beast doing all this while? He was very, very lonely in his palace, vainly waiting the return of his beloved Beauty. Every evening, at sunset, he would lie on the grass in his garden, thinking of her till his very heart ached with longing.

One evening, as Beauty sat with her father at their evening meal, a likeness of the Beast suddenly appeared before her, like a figure in a magic lantern. He was very pale, and looked dreadfully thin and woeful. Directly Beauty saw the vision she was touched with remorse and regretted that she had broken her word. The mournful eyes of the poor Beast, as they turned towards her, seemed to wear a look of reproach, and she remembered how kindly he had always treated her and what pains he had taken to gratify her slightest wish. This cut her to the heart; and that night, without saying a word to anyone, she laid the ring on the table when she went to bed.

When she awoke she was again in the Beast's palace; but no Beast appeared to welcome her. She had dressed herself very carefully, hoping to please him, but hour after hour went by and he did not appear, until at last she became dreadfully alarmed. She ran into the courtyard thinking he might be there awaiting her coming; but he was not to be seen. Then she hurried up the great staircase, and looked into room after room; all were empty and silent, and the longer she searched the more she sorrowed, for the thought came to her that perhaps the poor Beast was dead.

Then she went into the garden, calling his name, and at length found poor Beast stretched out on the grass-plot close to the fountain, to all appearance dead. His eyes were closed, and he did not seem even to breathe.

Beauty had never known till now how fond she was of the Beast, and the prospect of losing him altogether was more than she could bear. She tried every effort to bring him back to life, kneeling beside him, and moistening his temples with water. Then she called him

She found poor Beast stretched out on the grass, to all
appearance dead.

every endearing name she could think of, and at last, in very despair, brought a large bowl of water and emptied it over his prostrate form. At this the Beast opened his eyes, a gleam of joy shot across his face, and he gasped:

'Have you come back at last, Beauty? I have waited long for you and despaired of every seeing you again. But now I have looked on you once more, I can die quite happily.'

'No! No!' cried Beauty. 'My own dear Beast, you must not die. You have been very kind to me – much kinder than I deserve – and you are so good that I do not care for your looks; and indeed – indeed – I – I would be your wife if you were twenty times as ugly!'

And she flung her arms round the Beast's neck, and kissed his great hairy cheek.

At this a great crash was heard. The palace was suddenly lit up from basement to roof, hundreds of most glorious lamps – blue, and yellow, and green, and red – gleaming like wondrous jewels. Then came a burst of music, delicious voices and instruments in harmony, and the whole scene was one of rejoicing and festivity. For a moment Beauty stood bewildered at the sudden change of scene; then a gentle, grateful pressure of her hand recalled her to herself, and she beheld, with astonishment, that the Beast had been transformed into a graceful and handsome young Prince, who was gazing upon her with mingled love and admiration.

Bowing low, the Prince said, 'Thank you, Beauty,' and began to say all sorts of sweet and tender things.

But Beauty was too startled at first to realize what had happened and interrupted him by exclaiming:

'But where is Beast? I do not know you. I want my Beast, my lovely Beast!'

The Prince answered her with eyes beaming with gratitude and affection.

'I am he, dear Beauty. A wicked fairy had laid me under a spell, and transformed me into the shape of a hideous beast, which I was to retain until a beautiful girl should consent, of her own free will, to marry me. You have done so: your goodness of heart and your gratitude made you overlook my ugliness; and in consenting to become the wife of the Beast you have restored an unfortunate Prince to his own shape and to happiness.'

Beauty, still greatly surprised, but radiant with happiness, let the Prince lead her back to his palace and summon her father.

Great was the astonishment of the two sisters when they heard that Beauty, whom they had laughed at and despised, was to marry a Prince; but all their astonishment did not alter the fact. Beauty was far too good and kind a girl to remember how shabbily they had treated her, and gave them a warm welcome at the wedding; but as they made themselves anything but agreeable, and still made spiteful remarks, a fairy who was present decreed that they should be turned into statues and stand at the door of Beauty's palace, so that they might find their punishment in beholding her happiness. Only when they repented would they become women again. For all we know they are there still, for they were certainly *very* disagreeable people.

The Babes in the Wood

ONCE upon a time there lived a good and wise Lord and a beautiful Lady. They had two dear little children – a fine boy and a very pretty girl. Their home was one of the happiest in all the land, for they loved one another dearly; and the father and mother, being noble and kind, had taught their children to be so too.

But soon great misfortunes came to this happy family.

First, the mother died, which was a great blow to the children. Then, a short time after, when the boy was only five years old and the little girl a year younger, their dear father was also taken away.

When the good Lord knew that his end was near, he sent for his brother; and, calling him to the bedside, said:

'Dear brother, I am dying. In a few short hours, or days at most, my poor little Babes will be alone in the world. Happily, I am able to leave them well provided for, and I have saved money enough for all their needs. I leave them to your care, since you are the only relative they have. Guard and cherish them, I beg you, for my sake! My son in years to come will have this castle, and money enough to keep up his proper state; and my daughter will have a sufficient fortune. I ask you, my brother, to take charge of everything until they are old enough to manage their own affairs. I beg you to promise that you will deal justly by them, and love them for my sake!'

'I will care for them as if they were my own!' said the younger Lord. A few hours later the good Lord died, well content.

A week or two after the funeral the Uncle took the two children away to his own castle to live with him, and at first treated them kindly.

At heart, however, he was a bad man, and quite unlike the good Lord who had passed away. He was greedy and cruel; and while he watched the helpless children at their play a cunning plan shaped itself in his mind by which he hoped to get rid of them, and thus be able to keep their money and lands for himself.

One night, late in autumn, he sent for two robbers, whom he knew to be bold and bad men, ready in return for money to do any cruel deed. He bade them take the two little children out into the forest next day and there kill them, promising them a large sum of money in return. The robbers agreed to do as he wished, and, very pleased at the prospect of getting money so easily, they sat drinking until late in the night.

Next morning the wicked Uncle came quite early to the room where the children slept. 'Rise,' he said, 'and dress quickly. Two friends of mine are going to take you for a stroll in the woods this fine morning.'

'But we haven't had our breakfast yet, and we're *so* hungry!' cried the little boy, remembering, also, that they had not had any supper the night before.

Next morning the wicked Uncle came quite early to the
room where the children slept.

'I don't like those big, ugly men! They frighten me!' cried the little girl, when they reached the hall where the two robbers were waiting.

She began to cry, but the wicked Uncle took no notice of either tears or words. The robbers took the children by the hand and dragged them away to the darkest part of the wood.

The poor little orphans were so frightened that they dared not even whisper to each other. When they came to the darkest part of the forest, and found that the robbers meant to kill them, they cried and cried, and, falling on their knees, begged for mercy.

So piteously did they plead that one of the men, whose heart was not quite so hard as that of his mate, felt suddenly a little sorry for the cruel deed he was about to do, and would have spared their lives. But his companion would not hear of this, and cried angrily, 'Do not be a fool, man! Let us kill the brats, or else we shall not get the reward!'

The other robber, however, still wished to save the children; and at last the squabble between the two grew so fierce that they started to fight, drawing knives and rushing at each other desperately.

The two men fought for a long time, while the children sat helplessly on a tree-trunk, fearing to run away lest the cruel knives should be plunged into their own breasts.

At last the cruellest robber was killed. The other then took the trembling children by the hand and led them on again. When they had reached the most lonely part of the forest, he made them sit down under a tree, and said to them, 'Stay here a short time and rest, little ones, while I go to find some food for you! I will not be long!'

He soon disappeared among the trees, and quickly made his way to the path, since he had not the slightest intention of returning to the children again. When he got back to the castle of the wicked Uncle, he declared that the little boy and his sister were dead, and claimed the promised reward. The bad Lord was glad to hear that he might now claim the estates of his dead brother, and willingly paid over the money to the robber, who took it and returned to his usual evil way of living.

Meanwhile, the poor Babes sat under the tree and patiently awaited the robber's return. After several hours had passed they felt sure he did not mean to return to them, and the little boy said:

'We are left alone, little sister, and we must try to find our way out of this dreadful forest as best we can!'

The little girl began to cry, for she was already so tired and hungry that she felt she could hardly move; but her brother took her by the hand, bravely keeping back his own tears, and together they wandered through the dense wood, trying to find a path that would take them out.

But every step they took led them farther into the forest; and at last the sun went down and night came on.

Then, as the stars came out one by one, the little girl cried:

'I can go no farther, dear brother! Oh, must we stay all night in this dreadful forest?'

'I'm afraid so, little sister!' replied the boy, adding with a brave smile, 'But it is not really so dreadful, after all. See, there are the dear little stars twinkling above us.'

They were now in a deep, sheltered glade, and, too hungry and worn out to go another step, they threw

The two men fought for a long time, while the children
sat helplessly on a tree-trunk.

themselves down on a soft mossy bank. With their little arms lovingly twined round each other, and their pale cheeks closely pressed together, they soon fell asleep. Two dear little squirrels perched on the tree above stood as sentries over them all night; and the sweet song of a nightingale lulled them to sleep. They dreamt of their dear father and mother; and, as the night wore on, a sweet smile of peace stole over the faces of the two little sleepers.

When dawn came and the golden sunlight streamed through the over-hanging trees, the two sweet Babes still lay locked in each other's arms. The sun climbed higher and higher, but still they did not stir nor open their eyes, for they had died in their sleep, and all their troubles were at an end.

When the robin-redbreasts and the squirrels looked down on the little brother and sister, they knew that they were dead; and as the birds could not dig a grave for them, they brought the autumn-tinted leaves in their bills and showered them over the still forms which lay upon the ground.

Quickly and quietly the little workers performed their labour of love; and, ere long, the two Babes were covered with a soft pall of autumn leaves. Then the robins sang a mournful song, and the squirrels and the rabbits felt so sad that they would not gambol or play any more that day.

As for the wicked Uncle, he did not long enjoy his ill-gotten gains. From that day no luck came to him. The robber who had left the children to die in the wood was condemned to death for another crime, and made a full confession of his misdeeds, so that the sad story of the poor Babes in the Wood was known all through the countryside. People would have nothing further to do with the wicked Uncle; little by little he lost all his ill-gotten wealth and died at last in great poverty.

THE END